W9-BFV-930

THE SISTERS
GRIMM

THE S
GRL

10th Anniversary Edition

1

THE FAIRY-TALE DETECTIVES

MICHAEL BUCKLEY

Pictures by PETER FERGUSON

AMULET BOOKS NEW YORK

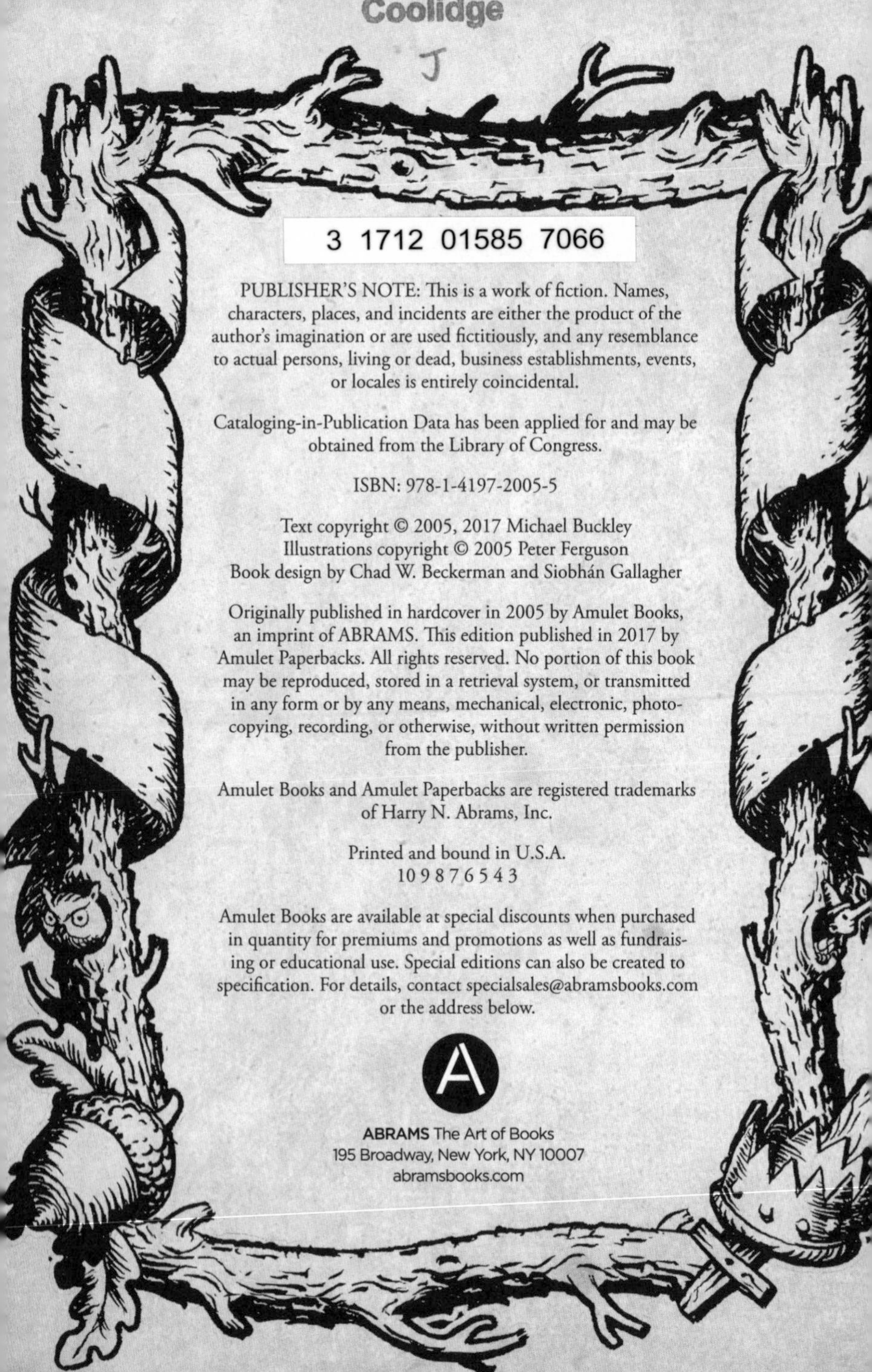

PUBLISHER'S NOTE: This is a work of fiction. Names, characters, places, and incidents are either the product of the author's imagination or are used fictitiously, and any resemblance to actual persons, living or dead, business establishments, events, or locales is entirely coincidental.

Cataloging-in-Publication Data has been applied for and may be obtained from the Library of Congress.

ISBN: 978-1-4197-2005-5

Book design by Chad W. Beckerman and Siobhán Gallagher

Printed and bound in U.S.A.
10 9 8 7 6 5 4 3

ABRAMS The Art of Books
195 Broadway, New York, NY 10007
abramsbooks.com

In memory of my grandparents,

Basil and Relda Gandee

In the distance a thunderous bellow rang out, followed by the terrible sound of falling trees and a stampede of terrified animals. It was coming, and there was no way to outrun it. Still, Sabrina and Daphne had to try. They sprinted as fast as they could, fighting with every step the dense forest branches that scratched at their faces and arms.

"We have to find a way to stop it!" Daphne cried between gasps.

Sabrina knew her little sister was right. But how? They were two children versus a vicious monster.

"I'll think of something," she said, dragging her sister behind an enormous oak tree for a much-needed rest. Sabrina squeezed Daphne's hand to reassure her while she forced air into her own burning lungs. Her words sounded empty in her ears. She didn't have a plan, and even if she did, it wouldn't make a difference. The creature was on top of them.

Splintering wood and damp soil rained from the sky as the tree they crouched behind was violently uprooted. The two girls looked up into the horrible face above them and felt scorching breath blow through their hair. What has happened to our lives? *Sabrina wondered. When did the world become unrecognizable? And what had happened to her, the eleven-year-old girl who only two days prior had been an orphan on a train?*

1

Two Days Earlier

I'M GOING TO DIE OF BOREDOM HERE, SABRINA GRIMM thought as she looked out the train window at Ferryport Landing, New York, approaching in the distance. The little town seemed to be made mostly of hills and trees next to the cold, gray Hudson River. Endless acres of evergreen forest surrounded it, as if trying to hide its existence from the rest of the world. A few two- and three-story buildings huddled around what appeared to be the town's only street. Sabrina couldn't see any movie theaters, malls, or museums, and she felt using the word *town* to describe Ferryport Landing was a bit of a stretch.

The weather wasn't helping. It was raining, and rain always made her melancholy. It had been raining the day her parents abandoned her a year and a half ago, and it still made her heart ache. She remembered the day clearly, rushing home that afternoon with a report card safely tucked inside her raincoat. Excited about her As in math and English and her B in science (and a little disappointed by her C– in gym). She proudly taped her grades to the refrigerator for everyone to see when they got home. It seemed odd that her parents weren't there, but Sabrina didn't worry until Daphne's kindergarten teacher called to find out why no one had picked up the little girl. That night the girls slept in their parents' bed, waiting for them to come home while thunder crashed in the sky outside. When the social workers came three days later to take them away, it was still raining, and Sabrina's report card was still hanging on the refrigerator awaiting its praise. For all Sabrina knew, it was still there.

The police investigated the disappearance. They searched the family's New York City apartment for clues. They interviewed neighbors and coworkers. They dusted for fingerprints and filed reports, but Henry and Veronica Grimm had vanished into thin air. Months later the police found their abandoned car, deserted in a lonely park fifty miles north of the city. The only clue was a bloodred handprint on the dashboard that turned out to be paint but didn't lead to anything else. The investigation came to a dead end, and the cops eventually gave up the search.

The girls were placed under the care of social services at first. A nice but overworked man named Todd searched for a next of kin, someone who could take them in, but came up as empty as the police. No aunts, uncles, grandparents, brothers, sisters, or even distant twice-removed cousins existed. Todd promised to keep trying, but when Sabrina and Daphne were moved to an orphanage, they never saw him again.

Sabrina shook off the sad memories and tucked her long blond hair behind her ear. She felt like crying but couldn't let her sister see her blubbering. She needed to be the strong one; after all, she was almost twelve years old.

Not that Daphne would have noticed. At the moment, Sabrina's seven-year-old sister had her face pressed against the train's window, as she had for the entire two-hour trip. She marveled at each ugly little dot on the map they rolled through like they were Paris, Rome, and Los Angeles. She only took occasional breaks from the view to ask questions about their destination.

"Do they have bagels in Ferryport Landing, Ms. Smirt?" Daphne asked the woman sitting across from them. Ms. Minerva Smirt was the girls' caseworker from the orphanage. She was a pinch-lipped, humorless woman in her late fifties. As usual, her hooked nose was buried in a book. Sabrina knew she was reading only so she wouldn't have to talk to them.

Ms. Smirt looked up at Daphne with an annoyed scowl and sighed as if the little girl's questions were more than she could bear.

"Of course they have bagels. They have bagels everywhere," Ms. Smirt snapped.

"Not on the moon," Daphne replied matter-of-factly as she returned her gaze to the window.

Ms. Smirt snarled, and Sabrina snickered. It was so easy to get on the woman's nerves, and Daphne was particularly good at it. Smirt had made a terrible mistake when she chose a career working with children, Sabrina thought, especially since she didn't seem to like them. The woman complained whenever she had to touch their sticky hands or wipe their runny noses, and reading bedtime stories was completely out of the question. She seemed to especially dislike the Grimm sisters, labeling them rude, uncooperative, and a couple of know-it-alls. So Sabrina was sure it was Ms. Smirt's personal mission to get the girls out of the orphanage and into a foster home. So far she had failed miserably, sending them to live with people who were usually mean and occasionally crazy. Some used them as maids and house sitters, while others just plain ignored them. This time, however, Smirt had gone too far. This time she was sending them to live with a dead woman.

"I hope you won't bother your grandmother with all these ridiculous questions!" Ms. Smirt said curtly, which was how she said most things to Sabrina and Daphne. "She is old and cannot handle a lot of trouble."

"She's dead! I've already told you a million times, our grandmother is dead!" said Sabrina.

"We did a background check, Sally," Ms. Smirt replied. "She is who she says she is."

"My name is Sabrina." Sabrina sighed.

"Whatever. The orphanage would not just release you into anyone's custody," said Ms. Smirt.

"Oh, really? How about Ms. Langdon, who swore her toilet was haunted?" said Sabrina.

"Everyone has their quirks."

"Or Mr. Dennison, who made us sleep in his truck?" Daphne chimed in.

"Some people love the great outdoors."

"Mr. and Mrs. Johnson handcuffed us to a radiator!" Sabrina cried.

Ms. Smirt rolled her eyes. "You act like it was the end of the world. Imagine how hard this has been on me. I was mortified when I heard what you said to the Keatons!"

"They locked us in their house for two weeks so they could go on a cruise to Bora-Bora," Sabrina said.

"I think it was the Bahamas," Daphne said.

"It was Bermuda, and they brought you both back some lovely T-shirts," said Ms. Smirt. "Anyway, it's all water under the bridge now. We found a real relative who is actually eager to take you into her home, and not a moment too soon. To be honest, we have run out of families looking for rude little girls. Even if she were an imposter, I would hand you over to her. "

With that, Ms. Smirt put her nose back into her book. Sabrina looked at the title. It was called *How to Get the Love You Want.*

The conductor's voice rang out from the speakers on the ceiling. He announced that Ferryport Landing was the next and last stop.

"What's an imposter?" Daphne asked.

"It's a person who pretends to be someone she's not," Sabrina said.

"Do you think there's any chance she's really our grandmother?"

"Not a chance," Sabrina whispered into her sister's ear. "Dad told me she died before we were even born. No, she's some crackpot, but don't worry—we'll be gone before the crazy old bat knows what's happened."

The train slowed as it pulled into the station, and passengers got up from their seats. They took down their bags from the luggage racks above and tossed half-read newspapers onto the coffee-stained floor before heading toward the doors.

"Ladies, let's go!" Ms. Smirt ordered. Sabrina didn't want to meet this imposter, but she knew better than to argue with the old crone. Smirt had a reputation as a pincher, and she'd left more than a few nasty purple bruises on back-talking orphans. So Sabrina did as she was told and dragged Daphne's and her tiny suitcases down from the rack, then followed Ms. Smirt and her sister off the train.

The rain was bitingly cold. Daphne shivered, so Sabrina wrapped her arm around her sister's shoulders and held her tightly as they disembarked onto the crowded platform.

"The two of you had better be polite, or there's going to be trouble," Ms. Smirt said. "No sass, no back talk, stand up straight, and act like young ladies for once, or so help me I'll—"

"Ms. Smirt?" A chubby old woman interrupted the caseworker's threat. She was dressed in an ankle-length navy-blue dress and had a white knitted shawl around her shoulders. Her gray hair was streaked with red, hinting at its original color, and she wore it tightly tucked under a matching navy-blue hat with an appliqué of a big fuzzy sunflower in the middle. Her face was a collection of wrinkles and sagging skin. Nevertheless, there was something youthful about her. Perhaps it was her red cheeks and clear green eyes.

Next to her stood the skinniest man Sabrina had ever seen. He wore a dark pin-striped suit that was several sizes too big and held a wide umbrella in one hand and his hat in the other. His head was full of untamed platinum hair, and his enormous, watery eyes were hidden beneath wild, unkempt brows.

"Yes, Mrs. Grimm. It's us," Ms. Smirt said, forcing her usual frown into a smile.

"Sabrina? Daphne?" the woman cried with a hint of a German accent. "Oh, you are both so beautiful. What little darlings! I'm

your Grandmother Grimm." She wrapped her arms around the girls and pulled them close. The girls squirmed to escape, but the old woman was like an over-affectionate octopus.

"Mrs. Grimm, it's so nice to meet you," Ms. Smirt interrupted. "I'm Minerva Smirt. We spoke on the phone."

The old woman raised herself up to her full height, which wasn't very high, and cocked an eyebrow at the caseworker. Sabrina could have sworn she saw the old woman smirk.

"It's nice to meet you, too," said Mrs. Grimm stiffly.

"I am just so thrilled to have helped you and the girls reunite."

"Oh, I'm sure you are," Mrs. Grimm said, turning her back on the caseworker and giving the girls a wink. She placed a hand on each girl's shoulder and turned them toward her companion.

"Girls, this is Mr. Canis. He helps me take care of our house and other matters. He lives with us, too, and he'll be helping me look after you," she said.

Daphne and Sabrina stared up into the old man's gaunt face. He was so frail it seemed as though the umbrella he was holding might collapse on him at any moment. He nodded, silent as a statue, then handed Mrs. Grimm the umbrella. He took the two suitcases from Sabrina and walked down the platform toward the parking lot.

"Well, ladies, this looks like good-bye," said Ms. Smirt. She stepped forward and limply hugged Daphne, whispering something in her ear that made the little girl cringe. Then she hooked

Sabrina in her uncomfortable embrace. "Let's make this the last time we see each other."

She gave Sabrina a final, painful pinch before the girl could pull away, then turned back to the old woman.

"Good luck, Mrs. Grimm." She reached out to shake Mrs. Grimm's hand, but the old woman looked at it as if the caseworker were trying to give her something smelly and dead. Smirt sensed her disapproval, hemmed and hawed for a moment, then quickly reboarded the train without looking back. The doors shut, and soon it pulled away, back to New York City.

Mrs. Grimm directed the girls down the platform, unloading a barrage of kisses that continued all the way to the parking lot. Mr. Canis was waiting there, next to a rusty heap of a car that squealed in protest when he opened the back door.

"Is this safe?" Sabrina asked.

"It got us here." The old woman laughed. "I suppose it will get us back."

The girls crawled inside to find the interior was as ancient and shabby as the outside. Springs and foam erupted through the seat cushions, and when Sabrina looked down she could see a hole in the floorboard that revealed the pavement below.

"Put on your seat belts," Mrs. Grimm said.

The girls searched for the belts but found just two ends of a frayed rope buried in the seats.

"These?" Daphne asked.

Mrs. Grimm reached around, tied both ends together over their laps, and then smiled.

"There! Safety first," she cried.

Mr. Canis started the engine, and it sputtered, backfired, and then roared to life, belching a black fog out of the tailpipe. When he put it into drive an orchestra of gears screamed so loudly that Sabrina thought she might go deaf. Daphne plugged her fingers into her ears.

Mrs. Grimm turned to the girls and shouted something Sabrina couldn't hear.

"What?" Sabrina shouted back.

"What?!" the old woman asked.

"I can't hear you!" Sabrina yelled.

"More than six!" the old woman replied.

"Six what?" Sabrina screamed.

"Probably!" The old woman laughed.

"I love dolphins, too!" Daphne exclaimed.

"Not since I hurt my toes!" Mrs. Grimm shouted.

Sabrina put her face in her hands and groaned.

They drove through the little town, which consisted of a two-lane road bordered by a couple of antiques stores, a bicycle shop, a police station and jail, a post office, a dentist, a restaurant named Old King Cole's, a toy store, and a beauty parlor. Mr. Canis made a left turn at the town's one and only stoplight, and within seconds they were cruising out of the town proper and into what Mrs. Grimm called "Ferryport Landing's farm country." As far as Sabrina could tell, the only crop this town grew was mud.

After a long drive, Mrs. Grimm's house came into view. It sat far up on a tree-speckled hill fifteen minutes away from the closest neighbor. It was short and squat, much like its owner, with two stories, a wraparound porch, and small windows framed by bright blue shutters. It was painted yellow and had fat green shrubs lining the cobblestone path that led to the front door. It might have looked cozy if not for the looming forest behind it. Branches hung over the roof as if the trees were preparing to swallow the house whole.

"You live in a dollhouse," Daphne declared, oblivious to the creepy woods.

Mrs. Grimm smiled, but Sabrina wasn't amused. The place was troubling and weird, and she felt as if she were being watched. She squinted into the dense trees, but if anyone was spying he or she was well hidden.

"Why do you live all the way out here?" she asked. New York City was a place where everyone lived on top of each other, and that was exactly how Sabrina liked it. Living out in the middle of nowhere was dangerous and suspicious.

"Oh, I like the peace and quiet," said Mrs. Grimm.

And there's no one to hear the screaming of children up here, Sabrina thought to herself.

Mr. Canis unlocked the car's huge musty trunk, pulled out the two tiny suitcases, and led everyone to the front door. The old woman followed closely behind, fumbling with her handbag until she fished out what might have been the largest key ring in the world. Hundreds of keys jangled on the ring, each different from the others: skeleton keys made from crystals, ancient brass keys, bright new silver keys in many sizes, and several that didn't look like keys at all.

"Wow! That's a lot of keys," Daphne said.

"That's a lot of locks," Sabrina added as she eyed the front door. There must have been a dozen bolts of all shapes and sizes.

Mrs. Grimm inserted one key after another until she had unlocked them all. Then she rapped her knuckles on the door three times and said, "We're home."

Daphne looked up at her sister for an explanation, but Sabrina had none. Instead, she twirled her finger around her ear and mouthed the word *crazy.*

"Let me take your coats, *lieblings,*" Mrs. Grimm said as they entered the house and she closed the door behind them, turning the locks one after another.

"*Liebling?*" Daphne asked.

"It's German for sweetheart," the old woman said. She opened the coat closet door, and several books tumbled to her feet. Mr. Canis quickly restacked them for her.

"Girls, I must warn you. I'm not much of a housekeeper," Mrs. Grimm said, then turned to Mr. Canis. "We'll have dinner in about an hour."

Mr. Canis nodded and without a word climbed the stairs with the girls' suitcases. A moment later he was gone.

"Is he your boyfriend?" Daphne asked the old woman.

Mrs. Grimm blushed and giggled. "Oh, dear, no. Mr. Canis and I are not courting. We are just good friends," she said.

"What does *courting* mean?" Daphne asked her sister.

"It's an old-fashioned word for dating," Sabrina replied.

"Ladies, let me give you the grand tour!" Mrs. Grimm led them into the living room. It was enormous, a much larger room than seemed possible in a cottage so small. Each wall was lined with shelves, stuffed with more books than Sabrina had ever seen. Stacks of them sat on the floor, the tables, and every other surface. A teapot perched precariously on a stack that looked as if it would fall over at any moment. Books were under the couch cushions, under the carpet. Several giant stacks stood in front of an old television, blocking the screen. On the spines Sabrina read the strangest titles: *Birds of Oz*, *An Apple a Day: The Autobiography of an Evil Queen*, and *Shoes, Toys, and Cookies: The Elvish Handcraft Tradition.*

Mrs. Grimm led them through another door to a room where they found a dining room table littered with even more books, some open and waiting to be read. Sabrina picked one up and rolled her eyes when she read the title: *365 Ways to Cook Dragon.*

The old woman led them from room to room, showing them where she kept the snacks in the white-tiled kitchen and how to get the rickety bathroom door to close. Sabrina pretended to be interested, but in reality she secretly "cased the joint." In each room she noted where the windows and doors were, eyed locks, and paid close attention to creaky floorboards. It was a habit she'd picked up in the orphanage and all their foster homes: She always looked for the easiest way out. But here she kept getting distracted by the odd books and the dozens of old black-and-white photographs that decorated the walls. Most of them were of a much younger Mrs. Grimm and a stocky, bearded man with a wide smile. There were pictures of them hiking in the jungle, standing on an icy glacier, scaling a mountain, and even riding camels in the desert. And then there were pictures of them in the house, and Mrs. Grimm was carrying a small child in a papoose while the bearded man stood next to her, proudly beaming at the camera.

Daphne walked over to one of the pictures and studied it closely.

"Who's this guy?" she asked

"That was your Opa Basil," Mrs. Grimm said wistfully.

"*Opa*?" Daphne asked.

"Grandfather, *liebling*. He passed on before you were born," she said.

"Is that your baby?" Daphne asked.

The old lady smiled; then her expression turned serious. "That's your papa," she said softly.

The little girl's eyes grew as big as the moon as she looked over at her sister, but Sabrina quickly dismissed the old woman's claim. "Babies all look the same. An old photo doesn't prove anything," she muttered.

"Oh, my, I've forgotten the cookies," Mrs. Grimm said as she dashed to the kitchen. In no time she returned with a plate of fresh chocolate-chip cookies. Daphne, of course, happily grabbed one and took a bite.

"These taste just like my mommy's," she exclaimed.

"Where do you think she got the recipe?" Mrs. Grimm said.

Sabrina refused to take a cookie, giving Mrs. Grimm an "I know what you're up to" look. She wasn't going to be bribed with sweets. The old woman shrugged and set the cookies on a stack of books.

"Oh! I should introduce you to Elvis," Mrs. Grimm continued, then let out a blasting whistle. Suddenly there was a great rumbling in the house. Books fell from their shelves, windows shook in their frames, and the plate of cookies slid to the floor before it could be saved. And then something enormous came charging through the room and right at them. It moved so quickly Sabrina couldn't tell what it was, and it pushed over lamps and chairs, leaped over an ottoman, and knocked the terrified girls to the ground. Sabrina screamed, sure they were about to be eaten by a bear or some kind of hairy rhinoceros, when much to her surprise a gooey tongue licked her cheek. She opened her eyes to find the friendly face of a giant dog.

"Elvis, please, get off of them," Mrs. Grimm said, half commanding and half laughing at the Great Dane. "He gets very excited around new people." The enormous dog gave Sabrina's face one last lick, leaving a long trail of drool, before sitting down next to the old woman, panting and wagging his immense tail.

"This is Elvis. He's a member of our little family and completely harmless if he likes you," said Mrs. Grimm, scratching the beast on his immense head. The dog licked the old woman on the cheek.

"And if he doesn't?" Sabrina asked as she climbed to her feet.

Daphne jumped up and threw her arms around the dog. "Oh, I love him! He's so cute!" She laughed as she covered the dog with her own kisses.

"This is the only boyfriend I have." Mrs. Grimm smiled. "And probably the smartest one I've ever had, too. Watch!"

Daphne stepped back, and she and Sabrina watched as Mrs.

Grimm put her hand out to Elvis. "Elvis, shake," she said, and the dog reached out a huge forepaw and placed it in her hand.

Daphne giggled.

"Play dead," Daphne said hopefully, and the dog fell stiffly over onto his side, the impact knocking a lamp off a table.

Mrs. Grimm laughed. "You two must be starving after your trip. I suppose I'd better get started with dinner. I hope spaghetti and meatballs is OK."

"I love spaghetti and meatballs!" Daphne cried as Elvis gave her a fresh lick.

"I know you do," Mrs. Grimm said with a wink. She disappeared into the kitchen, where she began rattling pots and pans.

"Don't get used to this place. We're not going to be here long," Sabrina said as she wiped the dog's goo off her cheek.

"Stop being a snot," Daphne said as she laid a huge smooch on Elvis. *Snot* was her favorite word lately. "She wouldn't hurt us. She's nice."

"That's why crazy people are so dangerous. You think they're *nice* until they're chaining you up in the garage," Sabrina replied. "And I am not being a snot."

"Yes, you are."

"No, I'm not."

"Yes, you are," Daphne insisted. "So what if she's a little weird? Anything is better than living at the orphanage, right?"

"We've been over this a million times. What if Mom and Dad come back for us? The first place they'll look is the orphanage. We need to stay there."

"They've been gone a long time," Daphne said. She walked over to the wall to examine the photograph the old woman claimed was of the girls' father. Sabrina joined her, and they both stared into the face of the rosy-cheeked baby.

"He looks like Dad," Daphne said.

"It's not him," Sabrina argued. "It can't be."

While dinner was being prepared, Mr. Canis cleared the big oak dining room table of enough books so everyone could eat comfortably. He left an exceptionally thick volume entitled *Architecture for Pigs* on Daphne's chair so the little girl could sit on it and reach her food. Then the trio waited patiently for Mrs. Grimm, who was making a thunderous racket in the kitchen. Mr. Canis closed his eyes and sat silently. Soon his stillness began to unnerve Sabrina. Was he a mute? Was there something wrong with him? In New York City, everyone talked, or rather everyone yelled at everyone, all the time. They never sat quietly with their eyes closed when people were around. It was rude.

"Did he die?" Daphne whispered after staring at him for some time.

Suddenly Mrs. Grimm came through the door with a big

copper pot and placed it on the table. She rushed back into the kitchen and returned with a plate of salad and set it in front of Mr. Canis. As soon as the plate hit the table, the old man opened his eyes and began to eat.

"How did you know I like spaghetti? It's my favorite!" Daphne said happily.

"I know lots of things about you, *liebling*. I am your *oma*," Mrs. Grimm replied.

"*Oma*?" Sabrina asked. "What's this weird language you keep speaking?"

"It means grandmother in German. That's where our family is from," Mrs. Grimm answered.

"My family is from the Upper East Side," Sabrina said stiffly.

"Your mother sent me letters from time to time. I know a great deal about you both. In fact, when I stopped getting them I knew that . . ." She sighed.

"That they'd abandoned us?" Daphne asked.

"Child, your mother and father didn't abandon you," Mrs. Grimm cried.

"Mrs. Grimm, I—" Daphne began.

"*Liebling*, I'm not Mrs. Grimm. I'm your grandmother," the old woman said. "You can call me Grandma or Oma, but never Mrs. Grimm, please."

"Can we call you Granny? I always wanted a granny," said

Daphne. Sabrina kicked her sharply under the table, and the little girl winced.

"Of course, I'll be your Granny Relda," the old woman said with a smile as she took the top off the pot.

Sabrina stared inside. She'd never seen spaghetti like this. The pasta was black, and the sauce was a bright orange color. It smelled sweet and spicy at the same time, and the meatballs, which were emerald green, were surely not made from any kind of meat Sabrina had ever tasted.

"It's a special recipe," Mrs. Grimm said as she dished some out for Daphne. "The sauce has a little curry in it, and the noodles are made with squid ink."

Sabrina was disgusted, which made her decision not to eat the old woman's food even easier. This sicko lied about being the girls' dead grandmother. Who knew what she'd yanked from under the kitchen sink and added to the recipe: arsenic, rat poison, clog remover? Clearly she was trying to kill them. Of course, before Sabrina could warn her, Daphne had dug in with gusto and already swallowed a third of her plate.

"So Mr. Canis says your suitcases were nearly empty. Don't you have any clothes?" Mrs. Grimm asked.

"The police kept them," Daphne said, shoveling a huge forkful of pasta into her mouth. "They said they were evidence."

"Kept them? That's crazy! What will they do with them?" She

looked at each of them and finally at Mr. Canis, who shrugged. "Well, we'll just go into town and pick you out new wardrobes. We can't have you running around naked all the time, can we? I mean, people will think we're nudists."

Daphne laughed to the point of snorting, but when she saw Sabrina's disapproving face, she stopped.

"I was thinking that we—" Mrs. Grimm started, but Sabrina interrupted.

"Who are you? And don't say you're our grandmother, because our grandmother is dead."

Mrs. Grimm shifted in her seat. Mr. Canis, obviously seeing the question as his cue to retire, got up, took his empty plate, and exited the room.

"But I am your grandmother, *liebling*," the old woman replied.

"Well, then why did our father tell us you died before we were born?"

"It's complicated, and I'm not sure it's time to discuss your father's decisions."

"Well, if you really were our grandmother, I would think you'd be happy to discuss it," Sabrina snapped.

"We are all just getting settled in, and we can talk about it later," Mrs. Grimm said. Her eyes dropped to her lap.

Sabrina leaped up from her seat, sending her fork clanging to the floor. "Fine! I'm tired. I'd like to go to bed."

Mrs. Grimm frowned. "Of course, *liebling.* Your room is upstairs. I will show you—"

"WE'LL FIND IT OURSELVES!"

Sabrina walked around the table, grabbed Daphne's hand, and dragged her from her chair.

"But I'm not done eating!" said Daphne.

"You're never done eating. Let's go!" Sabrina commanded.

She marched her sister through the house and up the stairs.

"You're being a snot," Daphne complained.

"I'm trying to protect us," Sabrina argued.

At the top of the stairs they found a long hallway with five closed doors, two on each side and one at the end. Sabrina yanked on the closest one, but it was locked tight. She turned and tried the door behind her. It opened to a bedroom decorated with dozens of wooden tribal masks, wild-eyed and smiling hideously. Two ancient swords were mounted on the wall alongside the masks, and there were pictures of Mrs. Grimm and her husband, Basil, everywhere. Like the ones downstairs, each photo was from a different part of the world. In one picture, Basil was standing at the top of an ancient stone temple; in another, the couple were guiding a gondola through what Sabrina guessed were Venetian canals. She closed the door and tried the next door.

Inside, Mr. Canis sat cross-legged on a woven mat on the floor, his hands resting on his knees. Several candles lit the nearly empty room, illuminating its sparse furnishings. There were no pictures or decorations at all. Mr. Canis opened his eyes to look at the girls, his eyebrows arched.

Sabrina slammed the door without apologizing. "What a nutcase," she muttered. The next door opened to reveal a queen-sized four-poster bed with their suitcases resting on top. Sabrina pulled Daphne inside and slammed this door, too.

"We should give her a chance. I like her!" said Daphne. She sat down on the bed and let out a *harrumph*.

"A chance to what? Kill us in our sleep? Feed us to that monster dog of hers? No way!" Sabrina said as she charged to the window and looked out at a back-porch roof below. She could probably jump off it and then to the ground, but Daphne might hurt herself. "While you were shoveling in those meatballs, did you ever think that they might be made from the last couple of kids she claimed she was related to?"

Daphne rolled her eyes. "You're gross!"

Sabrina scanned the bedroom, which had soft yellow walls, a slanted ceiling, and a fireplace. A red ten-speed bicycle stood in the corner, an old baseball mitt sat on a desk, and several model airplanes hung from the ceiling. There was a nightstand next to the bed, with an alarm clock perched on top. And on the walls were dozens of old photographs. A particularly large one showed two young boys staring out over the Hudson River.

"Want more proof that woman is an imposter? Look at this picture. If that's our dad, then who's this kid next to him? We don't have an uncle!"

"Do you hear that?" Daphne asked, moving toward the window.

Suddenly Sabrina heard a faint whistling sound, almost like a flute, coming from outside. She joined Daphne at the window and peered into the woods behind the house. At first she thought she had seen something or someone sitting in a tree, but when she rubbed her eyes for a clearer look there was no one there. Still the music continued.

"Where is that coming from?" Daphne asked.

Like an answer to her question, a little light flickered outside the window. Sabrina thought it was a lightning bug. It flew up to the glass as if it were trying to get a better view of her; then it was joined by another light. The two danced around each other, zipping excitedly back and forth in the air.

"They're so pretty," Daphne whispered as a dozen more lights joined the original two. Within seconds more joined them, until there were almost a hundred little lights blinking and flashing outside.

Sabrina reached up and unlocked the window. She wanted

to get a closer look, but as she unfastened the window's latch, the bedroom door opened with a crash. Startled, the sisters spun around and found Mr. Canis looming over them.

"You'll leave that window closed if you know what's good for you!" he growled.

2

MR. CANIS PUSHED THE GIRLS ASIDE AND locked the window. The little lights outside flew around, bounced off the glass several times, and buzzed as if in protest. A moment later they were gone, and the whistling sound faded away. Mr. Canis turned and stood over Sabrina.

"You are never to let anyone or anything inside this house," he said in a voice as low and scratchy as an angry dog's.

"It was just some lightning bugs," said Sabrina. Her face was hot and red with shock. Who was this man to think he could tell her what to do?

"The doors and windows stay closed. Do you understand?" Mr. Canis said.

The girls nodded.

He stalked out of the room, closing the door behind him. Sabrina stood dumbfounded, trying to comprehend what had just happened.

"What was that all about?" Daphne whispered, but Sabrina said nothing. She was too shaken by the encounter and didn't want her sister to hear the trembling in her voice.

There was a knock at the door, and Mrs. Grimm entered the room. "Have you settled in, *lieblings*?"

"Mr. Canis yelled at us," Daphne cried.

"I heard," the old woman said as she sat down on the bed. "Please don't be too upset with him. He can be a little grouchy, but he has your best interests at heart. Believe me, *lieblings*, we are both very happy to have you here, but there are a few rules you have to follow." She paused as she looked into Sabrina's face. "And I know that what I tell you might not make a lot of sense, but the rules are in place for a reason.

"First, never let anyone or anything into this house without asking Mr. Canis or me if it is OK," she said. Her tone was stern and serious and no longer that of the sweet old lady with a plate of cookies. "Second, there is a room down the hall that is locked. It's locked for a reason, and I ask that you stay away from it for the time being. We have a houseguest inside, and he enjoys his privacy. You might hear some unusual noises coming from his room, but just ignore them. Do you understand?"

The girls nodded.

"And third, I'd prefer that you stay out of the woods. As for the rest of the house, feel free to explore. You'll notice there are plenty of books to keep you occupied."

"Really? Books? I didn't notice," Sabrina said sarcastically.

"If worse comes to worst, we can always dig out that old TV," Mrs. Grimm continued, as if Sabrina hadn't spoken. "Do you have pajamas?"

Daphne opened one of the suitcases and pulled out two extra-large T-shirts that read BERMUDA IS FOR LOVERS.

"We have these," she said.

"OK, well, I guess they'll have to do," Mrs. Grimm said as she moved toward the door. "Good night, girls. I'm very happy to have you here. I hope pancakes for breakfast will suit you."

"Absolutely!" Daphne cheered.

The old woman gave her a wink and disappeared into the hall.

"She's nice," said Daphne.

"Everyone who offers you pancakes is nice." Sabrina clenched her fists. "But she's not fooling me. Get some sleep. We're running away—tonight."

Sabrina lay in bed staring at the ceiling, listening to her hungry belly grumble, and planning their getaway. With a little luck she and Daphne could hide in a neighbor's garage for a couple of days and then hitchhike back to New York City. Smirt would be furious to see them again. She might even act on her threat to skin them alive, but the girls needed to be at the orphanage when their mother and father returned.

When the moon was high in the window, Sabrina nudged her sister awake. "We have to go," she whispered.

Daphne sat up and rubbed her eyes, her face full of heartbreak. Why was she acting like such a baby? Sabrina wondered. Running away wasn't exactly a new experience for the two of them. The sisters Grimm had pulled off many daring escapes from foster parents in the past. They'd tied bedsheets together and climbed out of the Mercers' window one night, feeding the pit bull, Diablo, meatballs stuffed with cayenne pepper to keep him busy. And after the Johnsons ordered pizza, the girls had slipped into the backseat of the delivery boy's car and were miles away before anyone noticed. Mrs. Grimm was no different than any of the other crazies. Eventually Daphne would understand.

When they were dressed, Sabrina slowly opened the door and looked out into the hallway. It was empty—and as the two girls crept out with their tiny suitcases, she used her sneaking skills to their fullest. She led them on tiptoe down the stairs, being careful to step close to the wall to avoid making them creak. At the bottom, Sabrina carefully opened the closet door so the latch wouldn't click and the stack of books inside wouldn't fall over and wake the house. She snatched their coats and helped her sister put hers on, then crept to the front door. Sabrina was just thinking that this was the easiest escape ever, when she tried to turn the knob. The door was locked, and when she looked closely she saw something unusual that she hadn't noticed before.

"There's a keyhole on this side of the doorknob," she whispered. They were locked inside without a key. "We have to find another way out. Follow me."

The girls crept through the house. They tried all the downstairs windows only to discover each was nailed shut. They found a back door off the kitchen, but it was locked from the inside, too.

"This is insane," said Sabrina.

"Let's go back to bed," said Daphne.

"No. We have to get her keys."

The little girl cocked an eyebrow. "How are we going to do that?"

"They're in her purse," Sabrina whispered.

A second search of the house turned up nothing. Sabrina concluded the old woman's bag was in her bedroom, which meant they had to go in to get it.

They stood at Mrs. Grimm's bedroom door. Luckily, there were no locks on it. Sabrina slowly turned the knob, and the door swung open.

The old woman's room was weird during the day but downright creepy at night. The tribal masks glowed in the moonlight, and the mounted swords flashed ghostly light around the room. Mrs. Grimm snored comfortably in bed, unaware of their presence.

"Where's the purse?" Daphne said, only to have Sabrina's hand clamp over her mouth.

The old woman turned over, disturbed by the noise, but stayed asleep, and when it was safe, Sabrina let go of her sister's face.

"Keep it down," Sabrina whispered.

She scanned the room and spied the handbag in the moonlight, resting on a table on the far side of the bed. She looked at Daphne, pointed to herself with her free hand, and then pointed to the bag.

Daphne shrugged. She clearly had no intention of helping.

Sabrina took a small step forward to test for creaky floorboards and found them secure. *This is going to be easy*, she thought, but as her confidence was building, she noticed Daphne taking an interest in one of the masks on the wall. The little girl took it off its nail and held it against her face.

"Don't do that!" Sabrina whispered.

"Why not?"

"Put it back. Now!"

The little girl frowned but did as she was told.

"There! Are you happy?" she whispered. A split second later the mask fell off the wall, landed with a loud *clunk*, and rolled toward the bed. Both girls dove to the floor as Mrs. Grimm sat up.

"Who's there?" she asked. "Oh, it's you. What are you doing down there?"

Sabrina was sure they were caught, but the old woman leaned over, picked up the mask, and set it on the nightstand. "I'll have Mr. Canis give you a new nail tomorrow."

Then she fell back onto her pillow and within seconds was snoring as loudly as ever.

"You did that on purpose," Sabrina seethed at her sister.

Daphne stuck her tongue out in reply.

Sabrina reached for the bag, fished around inside it for the keys, then tiptoed back into the hallway with her sister behind her. Downstairs, she quietly went to work on the front-door lock. There were so many keys, it took a long time to find the right one, but eventually she heard the telling *click* of tumblers turning. The girls waited for several moments, sure that everyone else heard it, too, but when no sounds came from upstairs they stepped outside and closed the door behind them.

"Good-bye, dollhouse," Daphne said sadly as she ran her hand lovingly across the door.

"We'll go through the woods," Sabrina said.

"No way! The woods are creepy. Granny Relda told us to stay out of them," Daphne cried.

"We don't have any choice. We don't want anyone to see us on the road and call the police," Sabrina said, grabbing her sister's hand and dragging her around to the back of the house. There they stopped at the edge of the lawn and looked into the dark forest before them. Crooked limbs twisted and turned in painful directions. A chilly breeze whipped through them with a breathy moan. The trees themselves were horrible, mutated guardians that seemed to warn Sabrina not to step onto their land. She told herself it was just her overactive imagination, but she had the feeling that if they did step into the woods, the trees would eat them for dinner.

Behind them, Sabrina heard a surprised yelp and turned to find Elvis trotting in their direction. He planted himself between them and the trees and stared at them with as serious a face as he could muster.

"Go away, Elvis," Sabrina commanded, but the dog refused.

"See? He doesn't think we should go, either," said Daphne as she wrapped her arms around the big dog and kissed him on the mouth. But Sabrina's mind was made up. She pulled her sister away and into the woods. Elvis followed close behind, growling and whining with every step.

Inside the forest, everything was deadly still. There were no scurrying animals, and even the rustling branches and snapping twigs were suddenly silent. It was as if someone had turned the volume down on the world.

Suddenly a high-pitched note filled the air. It was exactly like the one they had heard earlier that night, and it seemed to come from deep inside the darkness.

"There's that music again," Daphne said.

Sabrina shrugged. "It's probably the wind."

Elvis whined loudly. Then he rushed to Sabrina and clamped his jaw onto her coat sleeve, trying to yank her back toward the house.

"Get lost, fleabag," Sabrina cried as she pulled away.

"He's trying to tell us something," said Daphne.

"Just ignore him. He'll go back when he gets bored," Sabrina said as something zipped past her eye. She turned to get a better look and saw it was a firefly, just like the ones outside their window earlier. The little bug fluttered around her head and then circled her body.

"Look, Daphne. Here's the big menacing invader Mr. Skin-and-Bones was afraid would get into the house." Sabrina laughed.

"Pretty," Daphne said, holding her hand out and inviting it to land in her palm.

Elvis let out a low growl and snapped his teeth.

"What's the matter, buddy?" Daphne said as she scratched the dog's ears, but this did nothing to soothe Elvis. The Great Dane howled menacingly and lunged at the lights.

"Hush up!" Sabrina ordered. He was going to wake Mrs. Grimm and Mr. Canis if he didn't calm down, but nothing she said quieted him.

"Sabrina," Daphne said. There was a nervous tremor in the

little girl's voice that pulled Sabrina's attention away from the dog.

"What's wrong?" Sabrina asked.

"It just bit me," Daphne said.

Sabrina turned to face her sister and saw Daphne's hand covering her nose, but what startled Sabrina was the fear in the little girl's eyes. It was the same look of terror she'd seen on her sister's face the morning after their parents disappeared, when they woke up in their bed, all alone.

"Let me see," said Sabrina.

Daphne removed her hand from her nose. It was covered in blood. Sabrina was shocked. Lightning bugs didn't bite! And at that exact moment, she felt a sting of her own that brought blood to the top of her hand.

"Ouch!" Daphne cried out. "I got bit again!" Blood trickled down her earlobe.

Sabrina rushed over and used her shirtsleeve to clean up the mess, but as she did the two bugs became ten and then a hundred and then a swarm that circled the girls—thousands of angry little lights, zipping back and forth, diving at their heads and arms. Elvis growled at the bugs, but they were not intimidated. As seconds passed, more of the little lights appeared.

"Cover your face with your hands and run!" Sabrina shouted.

Daphne did as she was told, and the two girls ran as fast as they could. Elvis stayed close to their heels, barking and howling. When Sabrina looked back, she saw the swarm was close behind, and before long they were overtaken. Daphne cried out and tripped over a tree root. She curled into a ball and tried to hide any exposed skin. Elvis leaped on top of the little girl, doing his best to cover her as the bugs dived, biting her uncovered hands and legs.

Sabrina waved her hands and screamed at the bugs, hoping to lure them away from her sister, and it worked. They instantly darted in her direction, so she turned to run, but before she could take a step she slammed into something solid and fell to the ground. It was Mrs. Grimm.

"We have to run, Mrs. Grimm!" Sabrina cried, but the old woman stood calmly, as if she were daring the bugs to come closer.

"It's OK, *liebling*," she said. "I'll handle this."

When the swarm was nearly on top of them, the old woman raised her hand to her mouth and blew a soft blue dust into the air. The bugs caught in the cloud froze in midflight, falling to the ground like snowflakes. The blue mist took out half of their number. The rest regrouped and hovered around them, as if debating whether to try a second attack. In one mass they darted deep into the woods and disappeared.

"That wasn't very nice!" Mrs. Grimm shouted into the forest.

"What were those things?" asked Sabrina.

The old woman turned to her and extended her other hand. "I'll need your help getting Daphne into the house."

Sabrina was sure the old woman would retaliate against them for running away. There was no telling if her craziness would extend to violence. Who could tell what a woman with swords hanging over her bed might do when she was angry? But Mrs. Grimm didn't seem angry at all. In fact, she looked genuinely concerned.

She asked Sabrina to undress her sister, then rushed into the bathroom and returned with a bottle of calamine lotion and some cotton balls. She applied the lotion to Daphne's bites and tucked the little girl into bed.

Mrs. Grimm wrapped her arms around Sabrina and gave her a big hug. "*Liebling*, it's OK now. You can stop crying."

Sabrina wiped her face and felt the tears on her hand. She hadn't known she was crying.

"Daphne will be fine in the morning—maybe itchy, but fine," Mrs. Grimm said as she handed the calamine lotion to Sabrina. "Pixies are harmless unless you are overwhelmed by them."

"Did you just say pixies?" Sabrina asked, unsure if the old woman was joking, but Mrs. Grimm didn't correct her. Instead, she wished her a good night and padded back to her room.

ღ

In the morning, Sabrina was so hungry she could have eaten her pillow. But she was still not going to eat Mrs. Grimm's food. She'd already cried like a baby in front of the old lady, and her weakness made her hate herself. She wasn't about to give up any more ground. She spent the next twenty minutes trying to explain her philosophy to her sister.

"Daphne, I'm telling you we have to stay strong. She's being nice to us so we'll lower our guard. One of these days there will be poison in those pancakes you like to eat three at a time."

"No one would do that to pancakes. Pancakes are sacred," Daphne argued.

"Do you really think she's playing by your rules? She told us that pixies attacked us last night. She's not right in the head."

"I have an idea," Daphne said. "Why don't we have breakfast, eat her cookies, play with Elvis, and enjoy this big comfy bed? She'll think she's won us over, and then one day, when she least expects it, like when it's time for us to go to college, we'll just go."

"You're not funny," Sabrina said.

"Yes, I am," Daphne said.

Mrs. Grimm called them down for breakfast, and the girls got dressed. As they approached the stairs, Sabrina heard a voice coming from the locked room across from Mrs. Grimm's. The houseguest the old woman mentioned was talking to someone—

maybe himself for all she knew. She put her head to the door, and the noise stopped.

"Did you hear someone talking in there?" Sabrina asked her sister.

"It was my belly. Pancakes!" Daphne grabbed Sabrina's hand and dragged her downstairs to the dining room. Much to Sabrina's relief, creepy Mr. Canis was nowhere to be seen. After several moments, Mrs. Grimm came out of the kitchen with a big plate of flapjacks.

"Good morning, ladies," she sang. "I hope you're feeling better. Anyone hungry?"

"I'm always hungry!" Daphne cheered as the old woman stacked three on her plate, along with a couple of sausage links, then turned to serve Sabrina, who couldn't stop her mouth from watering. She hadn't had pancakes since her parents disappeared, and her empty belly was telling her that no one was so evil as to poison pancakes. Still, she wasn't going to risk it.

"No thank you," Sabrina said.

Mrs. Grimm gave her a curious look.

"Hold on, *lieblings.* I forgot the syrup," the old woman said, rushing back into the kitchen. As soon as she was gone, Daphne looked underneath her pancakes, as if she were expecting a buried surprise.

"They're just pancakes," she said.

"You sound disappointed," Mrs. Grimm said, laughing, as she returned with a large gravy boat.

"Well, after last night's spaghetti I thought maybe you cooked like that all the time," Daphne said wistfully.

"Oh, *liebling*, I do." The old woman tilted the gravy boat over Daphne's pancakes and a sticky bright pink liquid spilled out. To Sabrina it looked like gelatin that hadn't set. When Daphne saw it, her eyes grew as wide as the pancakes on her plate.

"What's that?" she cried.

"Try it," Mrs. Grimm said with a grin.

Naturally, Daphne dug in, greedily wolfing down bite after bite. "It's delicious!" she exclaimed with a mouth full of food.

"It's a special recipe. It has marigolds in it, and wasp honey," Mrs. Grimm said proudly.

Sabrina looked at the funky, fizzing sauce on her sister's plate. It smelled faintly of peanut butter and mothballs. She was glad she had been strong.

"So perhaps we should discuss last night's excitement," said Mrs. Grimm as she sat down at the table and tucked a napkin into the front of her bright green dress. She gazed across at Sabrina and arched a questioning eyebrow.

"It wasn't my idea," Daphne said.

Sabrina scowled at her betrayal.

"Well, no harm done. No broken bones or anything," the old woman said.

"Granny, you have some mean bugs in your yard," Daphne said as she poured more of the syrup on her breakfast.

"I know, *liebling.* They sure are mean."

Suddenly a pounding came from upstairs.

"What's that hammering?" asked Sabrina.

"Mr. Canis is nailing your windows shut," Mrs. Grimm said as she took a bite of her breakfast.

"What?!" the girls said in shocked unison.

"I can't take any chances that something could get into the house or someone might try to get out," the old woman replied over the loud banging.

"So we're your prisoners?" Sabrina cried.

"Oh, you're just like your *opa.*" Mrs. Grimm laughed. "What a flare for the dramatic. We're just trying to keep you as safe as possible. Now, let's put it behind us. Today is a new day with a new adventure. This morning I received a call. There's been an incident that requires our attention. How exciting! You two haven't even been here a full day yet and already we're in the thick of it."

"In the thick of what?" Daphne asked as she placed a fat pat of green butter on her second stack of pancakes.

"You'll see. I don't want to ruin the surprise, but I do beg you to hurry with your breakfast. We need to get started right away."

The old woman got up from her chair, went into the living room, and came back with several shopping bags. She placed them next to the table.

"What is that?" Sabrina asked.

"Mr. Canis went to the store to buy you some clothing—just a couple of things to tide you over until we can go shopping."

Sabrina looked in the nearest bag. Inside were two pairs of bright blue pants with little hearts and balloons sewn onto them. There were two identical sweatshirts that were as awful as the pants—bright orange with a monkey in a tree on the front. Underneath the monkey were printed the words HANG IN THERE!

Sabrina groaned. "They're like clown clothes."

"Oh, I love them!" Daphne said, pulling the orange monkey sweatshirt out and hugging it like a new doll.

"Hurry, girls. We have to get going," Mrs. Grimm called.

After breakfast, the girls got dressed and looked at themselves in the bedroom mirror. They looked ridiculous. The colors clashed, and nothing fit. Daphne, of course, thought her crazy outfit was very hip, and she strutted around like a giddy fashion model. Sabrina, on the other hand, was sure Mr. Canis was trying to punish them for attempting to run away.

"I feel like a movie star," Daphne said as the girls hurried downstairs.

"You look like a mental patient," Sabrina remarked.

Moments later, they stood by the front door waiting for the old woman to collect her things. Mrs. Grimm rushed around the house, grabbing books off shelves and from underneath the couch, creating a tornado of dust that followed her from room to room. When she had collected as many as she could carry, she handed them to Sabrina. It was a heavy stack.

"Almost ready," she sang as she hurried up the stairs.

Sabrina looked down at the top book. It was titled *Fables and Folklore: The Complete Handbook*. Before she could question the book's purpose, she heard the old woman pull out her keys and unlock the mysterious door upstairs.

"She's going in to see the houseguest," Sabrina whispered to her sister. Daphne's eyes widened, and she bit the palm of her hand. For some reason Daphne did this whenever she was overly excited, and though it embarrassed Sabrina, she let it pass. The girl had a million little quirks, and she hung on to each ferociously.

"I wonder what he's like," Daphne whispered back.

"He's probably the last kid she adopted. She tied him up in there decades ago. He could have escaped, but his little brother stuck around for the pancakes. It's really tragic."

Daphne stuck out her tongue and gave her sister a raspberry.

"Shhh! She's talking to him," Sabrina said, straining to hear the conversation, but before she could make out anything, she heard Mrs. Grimm leave the room, lock the door, and head back down the stairs.

"Ladies, we're off," she said as she ushered them outside and went to work locking the front door. Then she knocked on the door three times and said, "We'll be back."

"Who are you talking to?" Sabrina asked.

"The house," Mrs. Grimm replied, as if this were a perfectly natural thing to do.

Daphne knocked on the door as well. "Good-bye," she said, causing her sister to sigh and roll her eyes.

As they turned toward the car, they found Mr. Canis standing on the path with Elvis at his side. He stared at the girls with a look of slight contempt.

"I have finished securing the windows," he said.

"Oh, good! Did you happen to speak to our neighbor?" Mrs. Grimm asked.

"We began a conversation," the old man grumbled. "He's not pleased."

"Well, he'll get used to them eventually, I suppose," Mrs. Grimm replied.

"He doesn't have a history of getting used to things," Mr. Canis said as they all climbed into the squeaky car.

"Who are you talking about?" Daphne asked.

"A friend. You'll meet him soon enough," Mrs. Grimm answered, then asked the girls to tie themselves into their seats. Once they were secure, Elvis laid his huge body across the girls' laps.

Mr. Canis started the engine, and the car rocked back and forth violently like a bronco trying to buck a cowboy. They backed out of the driveway and then cruised forward through a maze of desolate back roads and barren farmland. They passed an old dairy cow standing and munching hay by the side of the road. Mrs. Grimm leaned over and honked, then waved wildly at the cow as they passed. When Daphne giggled, the old woman told her how important it was to be friendly. Meanwhile, Sabrina was plotting her and Daphne's big escape, memorizing street names and calculating how long it would take to walk to the train station. She was still determined to run away the first chance they got.

The car came to a mailbox with the name APPLEBEE painted on it, and Mr. Canis turned down a long, leaf-covered driveway lined with ancient cedars, pines, and oaks. They passed a tractor sitting alone on a little hill and pulled over into a clearing where a massive pile of junk was marked off by yellow emergency tape. Wood, pipes, and glass were tumbled together into quite a mess. Mrs. Grimm looked at Mr. Canis and smiled.

"Well, we haven't dealt with something like this in a while, have we, Mr. Canis?" she asked.

The old man shook his head and helped her out of the car. Mrs. Grimm opened the back door, reached in, and scratched Elvis behind his ears.

"Girls, do you mind if I borrow my boyfriend for a moment?" she asked as she winked at Daphne.

The Great Dane crawled clumsily out of the car, stretched a little, and looked up at the old woman for instructions. She fumbled in her purse and took out a small piece of fabric. She held it under the dog's nose and he sniffed it deeply, then took off toward the pile of junk and rooted through the rubble.

"What are we doing here?" Sabrina asked.

"We're investigating a crime, of course," Mrs. Grimm said.

"Are you a police officer or something?" asked Daphne.

"Or something," the old woman said with a grin. "Why don't you two get out and take a look around? The more eyes we have the better."

She walked away and, like the dog, snooped through the pile of trash.

Having a two-hundred-pound dog lie on her lap had given Sabrina a cramp, so she and Daphne decided to get out and stretch their legs.

"She talks to the house, killer lightning bugs, and cows. Her food looks like it came out of a Play-Doh Fun Factory, and all the doors are locked from the inside. Now she thinks she's Sherlock Holmes," Sabrina muttered. "Still think she's a healthy old lady?"

"Maybe it's a game," Daphne said. "I'm going to be a detective, too! I'm going to be Scooby-Doo!"

Sabrina wanted to scold her sister again, but the look on Daphne's face stopped her. Daphne was having fun. The same light used to shine in her eyes when their father read her the Sunday comics or when their mother let her invade her closet to play dress-up. Sabrina liked seeing it there, and though it would make it harder for both of them when it was time to leave, she decided to let her sister enjoy herself today. Who knew how long it would be before she got the chance again?

Just then, a long white limousine pulled into the clearing. It was bright and shiny, with whitewall tires and a silver horse hood ornament. It parked next to Mrs. Grimm's car, and a little man got out of the driver's side. He couldn't have been more than three feet high. In fact, he was shorter than Daphne. He had a big, bulbous nose and a potbelly that the buttons of his black suit struggled to contain. But the most unusual thing about the man wasn't his size or his clothing. It was the pointy paper hat he wore on his head that read: I AM AN IDIOT. He rushed as quickly as he could to the other side of the car, opened the back door, and was met with a barrage of insults from a man inside.

"Mr. Seven, sometime today!" the man bellowed in an English accent. "Do you think I want to sit in this muggy car all afternoon?"

A tall man in a dark purple suit exited the limousine and looked around. He had a strong jaw, deep blue eyes, and shiny black hair. He was probably the best-looking man Sabrina had ever seen.

"What is this? Who are these people? Heads are going to roll, Mr. Seven," the man fumed as he looked around. "Heads are going to roll!"

"Yes, sir," Mr. Seven answered.

"I was told all of this was taken care of last night. It's just lucky that I realize that everyone who works for me is an incompetent boob, or we would never have known there was a mess out here until it was too late. My goodness, look at that rubbish sitting there in broad daylight. What do the Three think I pay them for? I can't have this nonsense going on right now. Doesn't everyone realize that the ball is tomorrow?"

The little man nodded in agreement.

His boss looked down at Sabrina and Daphne and scowled. "Look, the hobos are rummaging through the mess, and they're leaving their filthy children unsupervised. My goodness, man! As soon as we get back to the mansion we need to pass a new law making it illegal for children to wander around crime scenes."

"Very good, sir," said Mr. Seven as he took a spiral-bound pad and a pen from his jacket pocket and furiously jotted down his boss's instructions. His dunce cap slid down over his eyes, but he pushed it back into place and continued to write.

"Taking notes, Mr. Seven? I like your attitude. If you keep this up, we might be able to get rid of that hat," the man said.

"That would please me, sir."

I
AM
AN
IDIOT

"Let's not rush things, Mr. Seven. After all, you still haven't given these children my card. What did I tell you, man?"

"Give everyone your card. It's good networking."

"Indeed it is," the man replied, tapping his toe impatiently.

"So sorry, sir," Mr. Seven said as he rushed to the girls and shoved a business card into each sister's hand. It was purple with a golden crown on one side and the words MAYOR WILLIAM CHARMING—BORN TO LEAD YOU written on it in gold lettering.

"Now, what was I saying before I had to tell you how to do your job, Mr. Seven?"

Before the little man could answer, Sabrina stepped forward. If there was one thing she couldn't stand, it was a bully. "There should be a law against talking to people like they are morons!"

Mayor Charming eyed Sabrina for a long time.

"Where are your parents, child?" he finally snapped.

"We're here with our grandmother," Daphne answered.

"She's not our—"

Charming interrupted with a wave of his hand.

"And who is your grandmother?"

Daphne pointed to Mrs. Grimm, still busy rummaging through the junk pile.

The mayor growled between gritted teeth. "Relda Grimm is your grandmother? When will your cursed family die out? You're like a swarm of cockroaches!"

Mrs. Grimm looked over, saw Mayor Charming, and quickly came to join them.

"Good morning, Mayor. I see you've met my granddaughters. How goes the fund-raiser planning? It's in a couple of days, correct?"

"It is not a fund-raiser!" Charming bellowed, then took a deep breath to calm himself. "It's a *ball*! And it's tomorrow! Yes, I should be overseeing the final details, but unfortunately I am required to investigate every little stray cloud. As I suspected, there's nothing out here but a broken house. I don't know what the farmer expected with such shoddy workmanship. He's lucky to have crawled out alive."

Sabrina was stunned. He was right—the pile of debris was the remains of a house. Sabrina saw pieces of furniture and clothing sticking out of the pile and an old afghan quilt swinging from a stick in the breeze. What in the world had happened?

"So there was a survivor?" Mrs. Grimm said, writing in her notebook. "Girls, we've got ourselves a bona fide mystery!"

"Here she goes, Mr. Seven. Relda Grimm, private eye, out to solve the case that never was," the mayor said. "See, that's the problem with you Grimms. You can never quite grasp that in order to solve a mystery there must *be* a mystery. A farmer built a flimsy house and it fell down. It was an accident. Case closed."

"Then why did you call it a crime scene?" Sabrina piped up.

Charming turned and shot her a look that could have burned a hole through her. "You must have misheard me, child," he said between gritted teeth. "Mr. Seven, take down this note, please. New law—children should not ask questions of their elders."

"I heard you say it, too," Daphne said.

As the little man scribbled furiously in his notebook, Mrs. Grimm said, "We both know why we're here, Mayor."

Charming tugged on his necktie and adjusted his collar. "This is none of your concern, Relda."

"You know it is, William," Mrs. Grimm said.

Just then, Mr. Canis approached. Charming shook his head in disgust at the sight of him. "Well, if it isn't the big bad—"

"William!" said Mrs. Grimm angrily.

"Oh, did I say too much?" Charming said to Canis with a wicked grin, then leaned in close to the girls. "Do yourselves a favor, kids. Check Granny's teeth before you give her a good-night kiss."

"Do you think it wise to provoke me?" Mr. Canis said as he took a step toward the mayor. Despite the old man's skinny frame and watery eyes, his words seemed to unnerve Charming.

"That's enough!" Mrs. Grimm demanded. Her impatient tone shocked the girls, but the effect on the two grown men was even more startling. They backed away from each other like two schoolboys caught fighting on the playground.

"The dog has found something," Mr. Canis said gruffly. He placed an enormous green leaf in Mrs. Grimm's hand. It was nearly as wide as a suitcase, and the old woman's eyes lit up with wonder.

"Well, look at that, Mayor Charming. I think we've found a clue. There might be a mystery to solve here yet," she said.

"Congratulations! You found a leaf in the middle of all these trees," Charming scoffed. "I bet if you keep looking you might find a twig, or even an acorn!"

"You don't see a lot of beanstalk leaves in this part of the country," the old woman replied.

"Listen, Relda, stop meddling in our affairs, or you're going to regret it," said the mayor.

"If you don't want me meddling, then you must really do a better job of covering up your mistakes." Mrs. Grimm placed the leaf in Mayor Charming's hands.

The mayor tore it into a dozen pieces and tossed it into the air, then turned to Mr. Seven. "Get the door, you lumpy bag of foolishness!" he shouted. The little man nearly lost his paper hat as he rushed to the car door.

Within moments, they were gone. The limo spat gravel behind it as it drove away.

"Girls, why don't we take a walk over to that hill and sit by that tractor? I'd like to see this site from above," Mrs. Grimm said.

Daphne took the old woman's hand and helped her up the slope to where the lonely tractor was parked. Sabrina followed. When they reached the top, the old woman plopped on the ground and caught her breath. "Thank you, *liebling*. Either the hills are getting steeper or I'm getting older."

"Who was that man?" Daphne asked.

"Let's just say he's a royal pain," Mrs. Grimm replied. "Mr. Charming is the mayor of Ferryport Landing."

"What's with the bad attitude?" Sabrina asked. The mayor reminded her of the orphanage's lunch lady, who seemed to delight in telling the children they were getting fat.

"He can be a little grumpy," Mrs. Grimm agreed.

"He and Mr. Canis sure don't like each other," Daphne added.

"They have a long history," the old woman said as she stooped to pick a small black disk off the ground. "How interesting: a lens cap, from what looks like a very expensive video camera."

She dropped it into her handbag, then happily jotted down another note in her notebook.

"It's probably junk," Sabrina said.

"Maybe," Mrs. Grimm said. "Still, it could be a clue. A good detective is always looking for something other people don't see, that one thing that looks out of place. For instance, look at all the rubbish down there. Do you see anything that doesn't fit?"

"All I see is a house that fell down," Daphne replied.

"The mayor's theory is one explanation, but think bigger. What is surrounding the house?"

Sabrina made a deep, impatient sigh. Mayor Charming was rude and horrible, but he had a point. Mrs. Grimm wasn't a detective. She was just a busybody. This was a job for the police.

"Wait! I see something that looks wrong! The ground around the house is smashed down," Daphne said.

"Excellent eyes! And what could cause something like that to happen, Sabrina?"

"I don't know . . . Are we going to sit here all day?" Sabrina asked with a yawn.

"What do you think did it?" Daphne asked the old woman.

"A giant's foot," Mrs. Grimm answered. "Find a giant beanstalk leaf, and you'll probably find a giant."

Daphne laughed, but Sabrina was horrified. First pixies and now giants. The old woman was getting crazier by the second.

"I'd better go down and have a closer look. If you find anything that seems like a clue, let me know," the old woman said as she climbed to her feet. She gingerly walked back down the hill and joined Mr. Canis at the pile.

"She's funny." Daphne giggled.

"In the head," Sabrina grumbled. She eyed the field, wondering if she and Daphne might be able to make a run for it right then and there. No—she didn't have a clue where they were. They could wander the woods that circled the farm for days and days, and after their last trip into the woods she wasn't eager for a return visit. She needed to get a better sense of the town and its roads before she and her sister could make another escape attempt.

"I want to ride on the tractor!" Daphne cried, leaping up and pulling her sister with her. She dragged Sabrina to the rusty red tractor and begged to be helped into the seat. Sabrina hoisted her up, and Daphne grabbed the wheel and turned it, making *vroom-vroom* noises as she pretended to drive.

"Look at me—I'm a farmer," she said in a goofy voice.

Sabrina laughed and decided to play along. "What kind of food do you grow on this here land, Farmer Grimm?"

"Why, I grow candy on this here farm." Daphne laughed. "Bushels and bushels of candy. Just sent my crop to market last week. Got me a pretty penny, I did."

Sabrina smiled, even as a shadow drifted over her heart. Why had their mom and dad abandoned them? Didn't they realize the girls would be flung in every direction, never finding a place to call home, and forced to live with people who belonged in hospitals and prisons? Sure, Mrs. Grimm smiled a lot and made cookies and turned the day into an adventure with her make-believe, but that just made her the worst of the bunch. The security and dependability the old lady offered was tainted with crazy. She was like winning the lottery only to find out the money was counterfeit. Mrs. Grimm was the cruelest thing Ms. Smirt had ever done.

"Sabrina, look at the house," Daphne whispered. The little girl had stopped playing and now stared at the pile below.

"What? What do you see?" Sabrina studied the clearing but saw nothing new.

"Come up here, you have to see it from up here."

Sabrina crawled up onto the tractor and stood tall on its hood.

"There! Look all around the pile."

When Sabrina saw what her sister was so excited about, her heart leaped into her throat. The indentation surrounding the rubble had a shape.

"It's a footprint," she gasped.

3

SABRINA WAS SURE THERE WAS ONLY ONE explanation for everything she and Daphne saw that day. She and her sister were the butts of some elaborate joke. Mrs. Grimm and Mr. Canis were trying to make them look like fools. It explained why the old woman talked to the house and served her crazy food. It was why Mr. Canis nailed the windows shut. This was some kind of twisted joke.

When they got back to the house, Sabrina fully expected Mrs. Grimm to confess and reveal that she and Canis were pulling a gag. Unfortunately, the prank kept going when the old woman placed a weathered book in Sabrina's lap. It was called *Grimms' Fairy Tales*.

"So we've got a mystery on our hands, *lieblings*, and a good detective starts every case by doing research."

Sabrina handed the book back to the old woman. "OK, you've had your fun," she said. "Don't you think we're a little old to fall for your jokes? You know, we're not dumb. We know there's no such thing as giants."

Mrs. Grimm turned to Mr. Canis.

"It appears that Henry did not tell them," he said.

When the old woman looked back at the girls, a crease formed between her eyes and her face went pale.

"No wonder the two of you have been looking at me like I'm batty," she cried.

"What didn't Dad tell us?" Daphne asked.

Mrs. Grimm snatched the book from Sabrina and flipped through it like a maniac.

"This!" she said as she shoved the book back into Sabrina's hands. She jabbed her finger at the portraits of two old men. "Do you know who these men are?" she asked.

They didn't look familiar to Sabrina.

"Oh, dear," Mrs. Grimm said. "Girls, these men are Jacob and Wilhelm Grimm."

"They have our last name," Daphne said.

"That's because you're related to them, *liebling*. Wilhelm was your great-great-great-great-grandfather, and with his brother, Jacob, he wrote this book," said Mrs. Grimm as she pointed to the thinner of the two men. He had a large nose, tiny eyes, and long hair. "People call them the Brothers Grimm."

"We're related to the fairy-tale guys?" Daphne cried.

"Yes, *liebling*, the fairy-tale guys. But there is nothing in this book that's a fairy tale. These stories are their case files. The brothers were detectives, just like us. Every story in this book really happened."

"You might want to lie down, lady," Sabrina said. "You're talking crazy again."

"I am perfectly sane, Sabrina. Oh, how could Henry keep this from you? There's a whole family history you don't know anything about . . . All right, where do I start?

"OK, back when Jacob and Wilhelm were alive, Everafters were still living among humans," Mrs. Grimm continued.

"What are Everafters?" Daphne asked.

"That's what fairy-tale creatures call themselves, and they can be quite touchy about it. After all, *fairy-tale creatures* implies that they are all monsters or animals. Most of them are human, or once were, before a spell changed them. So, like I was saying, Everafters still lived side by side with human beings. Back then, you really could find an ogre living under a bridge, or fairies in the forest, or knights fighting a dragon. For thousands of years that was how everyone lived. Then things started to change. Humans grew afraid and suspicious of Everafters. I blame the trolls. You can eat only so many peasants before people start to get nervous. Tensions grew, violence swept the countryside, and laws were enacted that discriminated against Everafters. Magic was made illegal, and dragons were captured and caged. Some Everafters were run off their land or had their homes burned to the ground. Others were attacked in the streets, all because they were different."

"That's mean," Daphne said.

"Indeed! But people do terrible things when they're afraid. The brothers saw all of it happening and thought they could help. When something bad happened involving an Everafter, they helped solve the crime, hoping to clear the accused Everafter's name or to negotiate peace when the Everafter was guilty. They wrote down everything they witnessed and collected cases that occurred hundreds of years before they were born, and they put them all in this book. It's a reference guide for the next generation of Grimm detectives."

"Hardy-har-har," Sabrina said, holding the book out to the old woman. "Even if what you are saying is true—which it isn't—how did all the Everafters get to America? It says here that these two dudes lived in Germany."

"Eventually the brothers realized humans and Everafters couldn't live together any longer so they found ships and used their connections, and like generations of poor and persecuted people before them, the Everafters decided to move to America."

"Yay!" Daphne cheered.

"But America had its problems, too," Mrs. Grimm explained.

"Boo!" Daphne moaned.

"The brothers bought almost twenty thousand acres of rocky, unfarmable land on the Hudson River, the site of the future Ferryport Landing, and with the help of some magic and some hard work, they transformed it into this beautiful town. The Everafters built homes and settled in, and when things were going well, they sent word back to Europe. More Everafters came, some from as far as China and Russia. They joined the growing community, and for a long time everyone lived together in peace—that is until humans started moving into Ferryport Landing."

"Uh-oh," Daphne said.

Sabrina scowled. The woman's insane story had her sister listening with bated breath.

"By that time, Jacob had passed away and Wilhelm was left alone to convince the Everafters that there was nothing to worry about from their new neighbors, but many believed it was just a matter of time before they would be forced to move again. A few even called humanity an infestation and claimed that it needed to be rooted out. A rebellion grew, as did a plan to attack the neighboring town of Cold Spring to expand the Everafters' territory. Wilhelm knew innocent people would be killed, so he did something drastic that changed the town and our family's destiny forever. He asked for help from the most powerful witch in town, a dark Everafter named Baba Yaga. She agreed to help, and cast a spell on the entire town, circling it with an invisible wall, a barrier, locking every Everafter inside and stopping the attack."

"So it's a happy ending?" Daphne asked.

Mrs. Grimm shook her head gravely.

"No, Daphne." The old woman sighed. "Magic has a price. What it gives it also takes, and to get Baba Yaga to cast such a powerful spell, Wilhelm had to sacrifice something that was dear to him as well—our family's freedom. Our family is also trapped here. One member of our family must remain in this town at all times. If we all leave, or are killed, the Everafters will be free—including the very, very bad ones. It's why I couldn't come to the orphanage and get you myself. I'm the only Grimm in town—at least I was until you two arrived."

"Plot hole!" Sabrina shouted. "If you leave or die, the barrier comes down. So what keeps everyone in this town from killing you?"

Mrs. Grimm gave a quick look to Mr. Canis.

"I've made a few friends who look after me," she explained. "And many of the Everafters have grown to love this little town; they don't want anything to happen to jeopardize their presence here. They have married and started families, and some have begun small businesses—they have built lives in Ferryport Landing. A few have even given up their magical possessions in hopes of living a more normal life. And, with a couple of exceptions, things have been pretty peaceful in Ferryport Landing. But we stay forever vigilant. We watch the town, investigate anything strange or criminal, and document what we see, just like all the Grimms who came before us. You'll do the same, as will your children, and their children. We are Grimms, and this is what we do."

"But if it's the family responsibility, why did Dad leave it behind?" Daphne wondered.

"Your father met your mother and fell deeply in love. The two of them went back and forth from here to New York City while they courted. When they got married, they planned on living here full-time, but when his father died, Henry's grief was too much. Veronica was already pregnant with you, Sabrina, and the two of them decided that this life of ours was too dangerous. Henry wanted to protect you, even if it meant keeping our family legacy a secret and telling you I was dead."

Sabrina's blood boiled. This joke was no longer funny! "Don't talk about my mom and dad like you knew them!" she shouted. "You are not our grandmother! Our grandmother died before we were born! My dad told us so."

"Henry lied to you, *liebling.*"

"My father never told a lie in his life!" Sabrina was furious.

The old woman laughed. "It sounds like he hid more from you than the family history. *Liebling*, I suggest you take a look at that book and get to know the cases as best you can. Right now, I have some things to take care of upstairs. This evening we'll go to the hospital to see the poor farmer who owned that house. We'll investigate this crime, as Grimms have always done. I don't expect you to believe what I'm saying, *liebling*. I know it's a lot to take in at the moment. Perhaps Mr. Applebee will give you the proof you need to help you believe me. When you do, we will prepare you for what lies ahead. We are Grimms, Sabrina, and this is what we do."

She vanished up the stairs with Canis in tow. The girls could hear her jangling keys and knew she was opening the "off-limits" room with the mysterious houseguest.

"She's a lunatic," Sabrina whispered.

"She is not!" Daphne cried. "What's a lunatic?"

"Someone who can't tell the difference between a kid's story and the real world. Daphne, we can't stay here."

"You want to run away again? What if I don't want to go this time?"

"You don't get a say. Mom and Dad put me in charge when they weren't around, and you have to do what I tell you to do."

"You're not the boss of me." Daphne crossed her arms in front of her chest and huffed indignantly.

"We're out of here as soon as I see a chance," Sabrina declared.

After a dinner of purple meatloaf smothered in a pungent sauce that Daphne swore tasted like pizza, they were off to the hospital, with Mr. Canis again driving. Sabrina's stomach was grumbling, but she had once more refused the old woman's cooking; even if her theory about poisons in the food was contradicted by Daphne's continued survival, she wasn't going to risk it.

Once they arrived at the hospital, Mrs. Grimm said to the children, "OK, let's review what we know so far. It's important for detectives to review their clues. First, a farmhouse was destroyed by what appears to have been a giant's foot. A footprint surrounded the destruction. Second, a giant beanstalk leaf was found at the scene, a definitive sign of a giant. And it has been touched by a giant."

"How do you know that?" Daphne asked.

"Because Elvis smelled his scent on the leaf."

"How does Elvis know what a giant smells like?"

"Because," Mrs. Grimm said, pulling the brown fabric out of her handbag that she had held under the dog's nose that morning, "he smelled this. It's cloth from a giant's trousers. Take a sniff."

Daphne smelled the piece of cloth and looked as if she might be sick. "Egad!"

Sabrina declined the offer.

"Everything has its own particular smell, but giants are really stinky," the old woman explained. "Everybody and everything they touch will stink like them, too."

Sabrina shook her head and rolled her eyes.

"Of course, there's also the lens cap from a video camera we found on the hill overlooking the farm," the old woman continued. "My guess is the criminal wanted to videotape the giant when he arrived, though I'm still not certain why. And lastly, Mayor Charming showed up, and he's—"

"Is Mayor Charming an Everafter?"

"Why, yes, *liebling*. He's Prince Charming."

The little girl squealed in delight. "We met a celebrity!"

Mrs. Grimm chuckled, and then broke into a full laugh when she noticed the scowl on Mr. Canis's face.

"As I was saying, Mayor Charming showed up and tried to get us to quit our investigation," Mrs. Grimm continued. "If the house had really just fallen down like he said, he wouldn't have bothered to come by and check on it. He knows something he's not telling us."

"When he first showed up, he was angry that someone he called the Three hadn't done a good job cleaning up the place," Daphne offered.

"The Three isn't a person. They're a coven of witches: Glinda the Good Witch, Morgan le Fay, and the gingerbread house witch, Frau Pfefferkuchenhaus. They work for the mayor as magical advisors, but what they really do is sweep trouble under the carpet."

"I thought you said that Everafters gave up their magic," Sabrina snapped, hoping she had caught the old woman in a lie.

"No, I said some of them did. I'm sure there's plenty of stuff hidden away in closets and attics all over Ferryport Landing," Mrs. Grimm replied. "Including, apparently, a magic bean I wasn't aware even existed. Let's go inside."

Ferryport Landing Memorial Hospital was tiny, at least compared to the giant skyscraper hospitals Sabrina was familiar with in New York City. It had two floors and no ambulances in front of the emergency room door. They left Mr. Canis in the car and, as they headed inside, passed a short, squat man with two huge companions waiting by the hospital door. They were impeccably dressed in expensive suits, perfectly tailored to fit their extreme frames. The short man stared at Sabrina, sending a flash of heat to her face.

We look like idiots, Sabrina thought as she tried to tug her high-water pants down a little.

Inside, doctors and nurses rushed around the brightly lit hallways. The place smelled of cleaner and antiseptic. The three Grimms managed to maneuver through the chaos and approach the information desk, where a portly receptionist sat talking on the phone. His round face was friendly, and when he saw them he put the phone to his chest and smiled.

"Can I help you ladies?"

"We're here to see Mr. Applebee. He was in an accident recently," Mrs. Grimm said.

"Oh, yes, Thomas. He's in room 222," the receptionist replied. "Popular fellow. He just had three visitors."

Mrs. Grimm cocked an eyebrow. "Indeed? Where do I sign in?"

The receptionist handed the old woman a clipboard, and she signed her name. Before she handed it back, she quickly pointed out three names on the list to the girls: a Mr. William Charming, a Mr. Seven, and a Ms. Glinda South.

She rushed the girls down a hallway and through two double doors, then made a left, stopping at an elevator. She impatiently pushed the up button several times.

"Why are we rushing?" Sabrina asked.

"Because Charming is here to erase the farmer's memory!" the old woman said as the elevator doors slid open and they stepped inside.

"To do what?" Sabrina cried, but Mrs. Grimm ignored her question.

They got out on the second floor, found room 222, and hurried inside. On the bed was Thomas Applebee, a weathered old man with his left arm in a sling. His right leg was encased in plaster and held above the bed by a pulley system. Sabrina winced at how painful it looked and thought he was lucky to be asleep. Standing over him were Mayor Charming, Mr. Seven (still wearing his insulting hat), and a woman wearing a diamond tiara and a silver-and-gold dress. She was slowly emptying a bag of pink dust onto Mr. Applebee. When she saw Mrs. Grimm, she

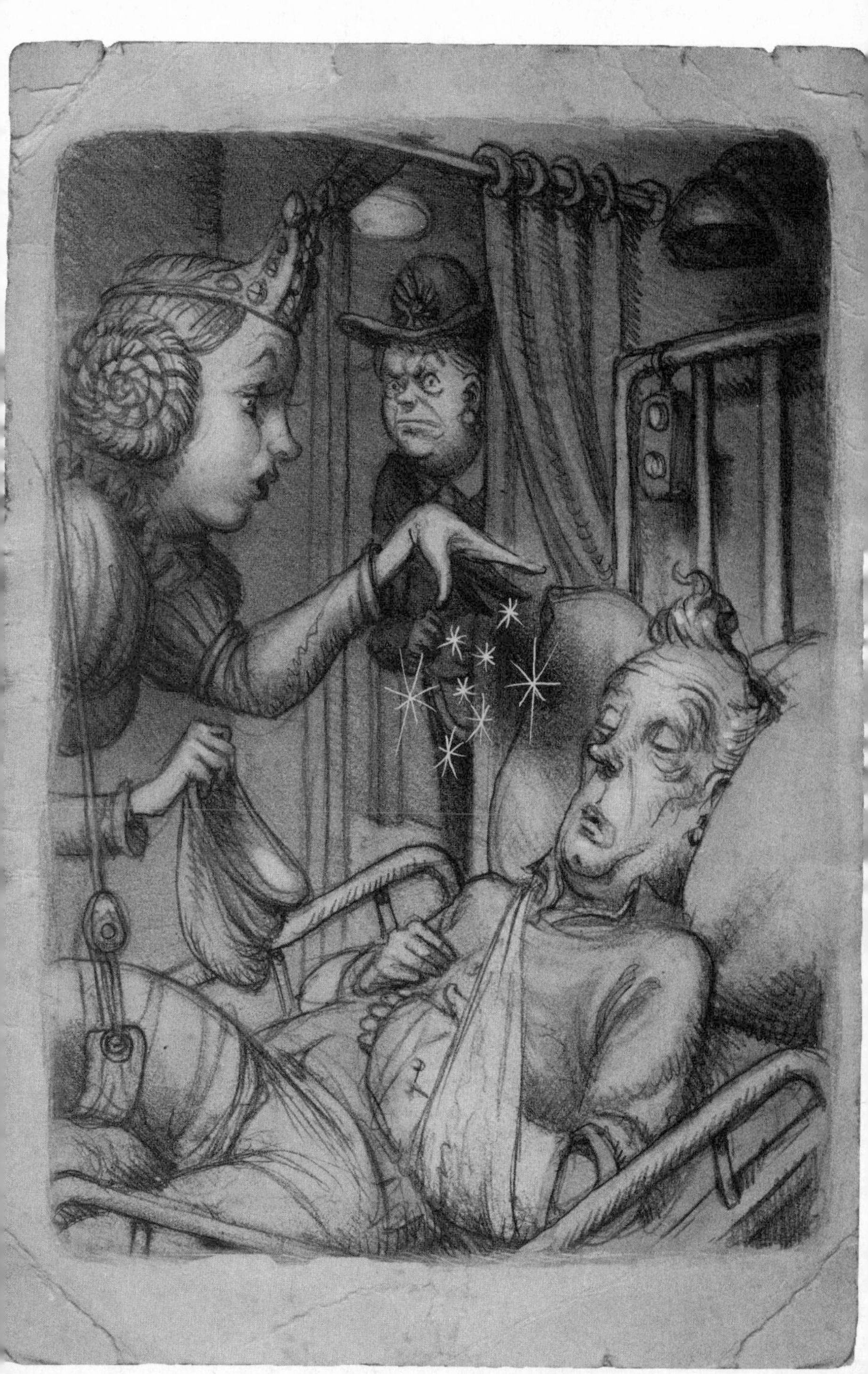

dumped the entire contents out all over the man and shoved the bag into her purse.

"Glinda!" Mrs. Grimm cried. "I thought you were supposed to be a good witch."

Glinda's face flushed bright red.

"We all have to pay our bills, Relda," she said as she lowered her head and quickly made her way to the door.

"Save your indignation," Charming added as he and Mr. Seven followed. "This is part of my job."

"Oh dear. Applebee will never be able to tell us anything," Relda Grimm said loudly, as if for the benefit of Charming and his team. "Without an eyewitness, we're never going to get to the bottom of this mystery."

She looked at the girls and pressed her finger to her lips so they would be quiet. After several seconds, she poked her head out of the room.

"They're gone."

"What are we doing here?" Sabrina asked. She didn't feel comfortable waiting around in the hospital room of a man she didn't even know. Especially since people were dumping what looked like the contents of vacuum cleaner bags all over him.

"We're waiting."

"For who?" Daphne asked, but no sooner had she said it than a thin, frail woman with gray-streaked black hair entered the room.

"Can I help you?" she asked, eyeing the old woman and the girls with some suspicion.

"Mrs. Applebee, I'm Relda Grimm, and these are my granddaughters, Sabrina and Daphne. We heard about the accident. Are you all right?" Mrs. Grimm asked.

"Oh, I'm fine. Thank you for asking. Do you know my husband?"

"No, but I happen to do a little detective work from time to time, and I was thinking I might be able to help. How is he?"

Mrs. Applebee gazed down at the injured man and smiled sadly. "To be honest, I'm a little worried about him. He was raving earlier. He told the wildest story. The doctors gave him a sedative to calm him down . . . Wait a minute, he's waking up," she said as he began to stir.

"Thomas, how are you feeling?" Mrs. Applebee asked as she sat next to his bed and rubbed his hand.

"Debra, who are these people?" the farmer asked his wife.

"They're with the police," Mrs. Applebee replied.

Mrs. Grimm stepped forward. "Not the police, dear. Detectives. It's kind of a hobby. My granddaughters and I are very glad to see you weren't too badly injured, considering . . ."

"You three are detectives?" Mr. Applebee looked from Mrs. Grimm to the children suspiciously.

"Yes," Mrs. Grimm said, causing Daphne to practically swell with pride.

"Well, I think a crime has been committed, Mrs. Grimm," Mr. Applebee said.

"You do?"

"They should arrest whoever dressed your granddaughters this morning."

"Thomas, be nice! I think they look adorable," Mrs. Applebee cried. "I'm sorry, he's been a grouch since we got here. He doesn't like hospitals."

Sabrina looked down at her goofy outfit and seethed with anger. *Who would buy a girl who was almost twelve a shirt with a monkey on it?*

"Well, what can I do for you, Mrs. Grimm?" Mr. Applebee grunted.

"Do you remember anything about the accident?" the old woman said.

"What accident?" the farmer asked.

Mrs. Grimm frowned.

"What accident!" Mrs. Applebee exclaimed. "Thomas, the house has been destroyed. I found you lying in the field unconscious. You don't remember?"

"I don't know what you're talking about. There's nothing wrong with the house," Mr. Applebee argued.

"Oh, dear, the painkillers are really doing a number on him," Mrs. Applebee said, shifting in her seat to face them. "Mrs.

Grimm, I don't think my husband is up to talking right now."

"I understand. Perhaps you might have a moment to spare us, then?"

"Of course." Mrs. Applebee gestured for them to follow her into the hallway.

"So sorry to trouble you," Mrs. Grimm said to the farmer as they walked toward the door. "I do hope you feel better soon, Mr. Applebee."

Daphne stopped and turned to the injured man. "I like my outfit," she said and stuck her tongue out.

Mr. Applebee stuck his tongue out, too, and the little girl stomped out of the room.

"He's acting very odd right now," Mrs. Applebee said when they were in the hallway. "I'm considering taking him out of this hospital."

"Oh, I'm sure he's in good hands. So you said he was raving about something," Mrs. Grimm prompted.

"It's silly. He swore he'd seen . . . well, this is crazy, but he said he'd seen a giant."

"He did?" Sabrina gasped.

"Wouldn't that be a sight." Mrs. Grimm chuckled.

"But I have a different theory about what happened," Mrs. Applebee explained. "There was a man who came out to the farm several times, asking us if we would rent the place to him for a night. He said he was making a movie, or something, and was very friendly at first, but when Thomas refused, he got quite nasty."

"How unfortunate. Has he come back?" Mrs. Grimm asked.

"Well, that's just it. A week later he did come back and apologized for being so rude. He said he wanted to make it up to us, so he booked us into a fancy hotel in New York City, all expenses paid, with tickets to a Broadway show. I haven't had a vacation in years—farming is a tough business—so I was thrilled."

"How nice. Did you enjoy your vacation?"

"Not at all. When I got there, I found that the hotel didn't have any record of our reservation, and the tickets to the show were counterfeit," Mrs. Applebee said angrily. "I should have stayed home with Thomas."

"Didn't your husband go with you?" Mrs. Grimm asked.

"Oh, no, he doesn't care for the city much." Mrs. Applebee sighed. "I took my sister. We had to use our own money for a hotel and the only place with a room was infested with bedbugs."

"How dreadful," Mrs. Grimm sympathized. "Mrs. Applebee, this man's name didn't happen to be Charming, did it?"

"Oh, no, it was Englishman," the woman replied, sniffing. "I remember, because Thomas said he had one of those accents they have over there. I thought it was a funny coincidence. You know, his last name and the accent."

"What did this Mr. Englishman look like?"

"I'm sorry, I never saw him. Thomas had all the dealings with him."

"Mrs. Applebee, I'm sure you want to get back to your husband, but I have one last question. Do either of you own a video camera?" Mrs. Grimm took a clean handkerchief out of her handbag and offered it to the woman. Sabrina noticed a soft, pink powder fell from it as the woman wiped her eyes. It was the same color as the stuff Glinda had dumped all over the farmer.

"No, no—Mr. Applebee is a little tight with the money, if you know what I mean."

Suddenly Sabrina noticed a change in the woman's face. It seemed to wipe itself of all emotion, and her eyes drifted into a blank stare.

"What were you saying?" she asked in a distant voice.

"I hear you had a wonderful time in New York City," Mrs. Grimm said. "The musical was the best thing you have ever experienced."

"OK," Mrs. Applebee said. Then she turned and went into her husband's room without saying good-bye.

Mrs. Grimm pulled her notebook out of her handbag and scribbled away. "So the plot thickens. More proof of our giant."

"That man is full of medications. He doesn't know what he's talking about. There's no such thing as giants!" Sabrina said, a bit louder than she meant to. The declaration echoed down the hospital hallway.

"Sabrina!" Daphne shouted.

"Listen, I don't know where you live, but my sister and I are here on Earth, where things can easily be explained without having to consider giants," Sabrina said in a much lower tone. "This Mr. Englishman wanted to rent their farm to make a movie. When the farmer wouldn't agree, he tried to trick them into leaving town so he could do it when they weren't around. Something went wrong on the set and he accidently blew the place up. Charming has an English accent. He's Englishman."

"Sabrina, I'm proud of you!" Mrs. Grimm said as she led them into the elevator. "You have incredible skills of deduction. You looked at the clues and chose the most likely path to solve the crime. You're going to make a great detective. But your theory only raises more questions. First, Charming isn't a filmmaker. Why would he want to videotape the farm? Secondly, what about the giant footprint?"

"Maybe Charming is making a campaign commercial. He is the mayor, after all. And as for the house, maybe it was a gas leak. Buildings blow up all the time in New York because someone left the stove burning."

"Brilliant! The town does have an election in the near future, so the campaign commercial is worth considering. And the gas leak is a valid theory. Still, there's one loose end. When things blow up, pieces fly everywhere. Applebee's house is all in a pile, like it was squashed from above," Mrs. Grimm pointed out.

The elevator stopped, and the Grimms stepped into the busy emergency room lobby.

"I agree with Granny. The house was stomped on," Daphne said.

Sabrina shot her an angry look.

"And I think I know who is responsible," said Mrs. Grimm.

"Really? Who?" Daphne squealed.

"I think you'll enjoy it more if it's a surprise."

"Excuse me, ladies," a voice said as three men emerged from the deep shadows that lined the pathway to the parking lot. They were the same men in suits who had watched them when they'd entered the hospital. The small dumpy one held a crowbar he kept smacking into his gloved hand. The men on either side of him stood like huge muscle-bound bookends to their much shorter leader. One glance told Sabrina the men were trouble.

"We hear you've been asking some questions about a certain farm," the dumpy leader continued.

"Then you've heard correctly," Mrs. Grimm said as she placed herself squarely between the girls and the thugs. Daphne grabbed her sister's hand and squeezed tightly, but Sabrina hardly noticed. She was too awestruck by the old woman's courage.

"Just a friendly warning, Relda. If you know what's good for you, you'll just forget about the whole thing," the leader said with a dark smile.

"If I knew what was good for me, I wouldn't be in this line of work," Mrs. Grimm replied. "I seem to be at a disadvantage, young man. You know my name, but I don't know yours. Or better yet, who the unfortunate employer is who hired the likes of you three. Tell him he should know it takes more than three goons to scare me. Now, good night."

She tried to pass the men, but as she did, the leader grabbed her arm and pulled her close to his fat face.

"Some people can't take a hint," he barked.

"Young man, if you don't let us pass, you are going to regret it," Mrs. Grimm said.

Sabrina's heart began to pound. How could Mrs. Grimm be so calm? These men were about to tear her apart!

"Is that so?" the head goon growled.

The old woman pulled a little silver whistle from around her neck and blew into it. No sound could be heard—it was broken. When she put it back inside her dress, she smiled.

"Yes, that's so."

4

LEAVE MY GRANDMOTHER ALONE!" DAPHNE commanded. Before Sabrina could stop her, the little girl had rushed forward and kicked the dumpy man in the shin. He cried out in pain and clutched his leg. Then Mrs. Grimm hit him on top of his head with her heavy, book-filled handbag, and he crumpled to the ground, groaning. Seeing how easily their leader had fallen to a little girl and an old lady, the two other thugs laughed.

"What are you laughing at?" the leader snapped as he crawled to his feet.

"Sorry, Tony," one of the goons said.

"Have you lost your mind?" Tony bellowed.

"What?" the goon asked defensively.

"You told her my name. We all agreed we were going to keep our identities secret."

The goon shrugged. "Sorry, Tony, I didn't think."

"Steve, you just did it again," the other thug pointed out.

"Shut up, Bobby!"

"Both of you shut up!" shouted Tony. "Why don't you idiots just give them our addresses and phone numbers, too?"

"Who cares?" Steve said.

"Because they can identify us to the cops," Tony complained as he turned his attention back to Mrs. Grimm. He raised his heavy crowbar above his head and snarled. "Now we have to do something drastic!"

"Easier said than done." The voice came from behind them.

Sabrina and Daphne turned to see Mr. Canis emerge from the shadows with Elvis close behind.

Steve laughed. "Look out—here comes her boyfriend."

"I'll make you an offer. If you run off now, no one will get hurt," Canis said. His voice was cold and hard, but the thugs just chuckled.

Even Sabrina could tell that frail old Mr. Canis wasn't going to be able to stop three thugs. He hardly looked strong enough to hold up the clothes he was wearing. No, the group was in big trouble. It was up to her. Sabrina searched around her for a weapon—a rock, a stick—anything she could use to fight the men. Unfortunately, the pathway was as clean of debris as it was of people.

"Girls, get behind Elvis, please," Mr. Canis said, taking their hands and pulling them back so that the Great Dane was between them and trouble.

"Enough of this. Get him!" Tony ordered, and Bobby and Steve lunged at Mr. Canis.

Sabrina was sure they had seen the last of the old man, but he caught both of the goons by the throat, one in each hand, and lifted them off the ground, holding them aloft as their feet dangled and kicked. Even more shocking was the loud, guttural growl the old man released when he tossed the thugs across the cold concrete ground. For ten yards they thumped and bounced, groaning with each painful smack against the pavement.

"All right, if that's the way you want to play it," Tony threatened. He pushed Mrs. Grimm roughly to the ground and swung his iron bar wildly at Mr. Canis. But the old man quickly stepped sideways and tripped him. He crashed to the pavement with his friends. Sabrina could hardly believe how agile the old man was, especially when Tony leaped up and rushed at him again, with the same painful results. She was doubly surprised.

"Hurry, girls—we should get to safety," Mrs. Grimm said as she got up and led them away from the fight. Elvis trotted along beside them, barking warnings at the goons not to follow. When they got to the car, Daphne climbed in but anxiously peered out the windows.

After several minutes, Mr. Canis was still not back. "We

shouldn't have left him," Daphne said. "There were three of them, Granny! He can't fight them all." Tears were running down her cheeks. Before Mrs. Grimm could calm her down, the car door opened and Mr. Canis crawled in behind the wheel. He was completely unharmed and wearing a little grin on his face.

"See, *lieblings*? He's just fine," the old woman said. She turned to Mr. Canis. "The girls were worried about you."

The old man turned in his seat and looked back at Sabrina and Daphne. He was his same painfully thin, watery-eyed old self. Daphne leaned forward and planted a kiss on his cheek. His face turned red with embarrassment.

"Don't you ever do that again!" she commanded as she hugged him tightly and then sat back into her seat.

Mr. Canis nodded in agreement.

"I, for one, am thrilled at what's transpiring," Mrs. Grimm said, taking out her notepad and pen. She began jotting notes frantically.

Sabrina was shocked. "Thrilled? We were almost killed."

"Killed? Oh, Mr. Canis, doesn't she remind you of Basil?" Mrs. Grimm tittered. Mr. Canis nodded.

"No, I think we have cause to celebrate," the old woman continued.

"Why, did you find a clue?" Daphne asked.

"No, not at all."

"Then what's to celebrate?" Sabrina asked.

"We're getting close to solving this case, *lieblings.* When they send the goons, the bad guys are getting nervous."

"So what now?" Daphne asked.

"We'll follow those hooligans back to their hideout."

"*What?* Why would we do that?" Sabrina cried, remembering Tony and his crowbar.

"Because they're going to lead us right back to their boss. Ladies, we're going on a stakeout."

Mr. Canis rolled down his window, stuck his head out into the cool night air, and put the car into gear. He seemed to instinctively know how to find the thugs' car. He trailed them at a distance (which was pretty great, considering the noise coming from Mrs. Grimm's old rust bucket), driving high into the hills overlooking Ferryport Landing. They passed no other cars, just a few deer that darted into the forest as soon as their headlights hit them. But Sabrina was in no mood to enjoy the scenery. Mrs. Grimm's sanity seemed to slip further away with every passing moment. Now the crazy old woman was stalking three dangerous men. It was clear to Sabrina that running away couldn't wait a second longer. They had to make a break for it the first chance they got.

Eventually Tony's car pulled into the empty driveway of a small mountain cabin. Mr. Canis pulled off the road as well, then turned the engine and lights off. As soon as they came to a stop, Mrs. Grimm fumbled through her handbag, taking out a pair of odd-looking binoculars with red lenses.

"What are those?" Daphne asked.

"They're called infrared goggles. They help me see in the dark," the old woman said as she handed them to Daphne. "Want to take a peek?"

Daphne raised them to her eyes. "Oh!" she exclaimed. "Terrifying!"

"What?" Sabrina looked out the window but saw nothing. "What do you see?" she asked nervously.

"You." The little girl giggled. "Here, take a look."

The older girl stuck out her tongue and took the goggles from her sister. When she looked through them, she saw the darkness illuminated in green light. She quickly spotted the three thugs going into the cabin.

"Is this really a good idea?" Sabrina asked. "Those men wanted to kill you at the hospital. If you don't care about yourself, shouldn't you at least be worried they might hurt us?"

"You are such a worrier. Let's sit for a bit and see who else turns up," Mrs. Grimm said. "Sabrina, would you mind letting Elvis out? He probably needs to stretch his legs."

Sabrina handed Mrs. Grimm the goggles and opened the door. Elvis lumbered out, causing the car to make noises that sounded like squeals of delight. It was the perfect time to run. The girls could use the woods for cover as they made their escape. But Daphne was leaning on the front seat asking questions.

"Granny Relda, are all the fairy tales true?"

"Almost all of them, but some are just bedtime stories to get kids to go to sleep. For instance, a dish never ran away with a spoon."

"How about the three little pigs?"

Mr. Canis shifted in his seat but said nothing.

"Yes, dear, they are real," Mrs. Grimm replied.

"How about Snow White?"

"She's a teacher at Ferryport Landing Elementary. We're going to enroll you two there in a couple of weeks. She's very sweet and, as you know, very good with little people like yourselves."

"What about Santa Claus?"

"I've never met him, but I have it on good faith that he is alive and well."

Sabrina poked her sister, but the little girl swatted her away, too caught up in the conversation to notice their perfect opportunity to make a run for it.

"I've got a question for you," Sabrina said. "These stories were written hundreds of years ago. How could all these people still be alive?"

"Magic," Mrs. Grimm explained, as if it were obvious.

"Yeah, magic. Duh!" Daphne said.

Sabrina shot her an angry look, but the little girl ignored it.

"Granny Relda, have you ever seen a giant?" Daphne asked.

"Of course, *liebling*, I've even been to the giant kingdom on a couple of occasions. The last time, I was nearly squished by the Giant Queen's toe." Mrs. Grimm laughed.

"Well, if there really are giants, how come we haven't seen any yet?" Daphne asked.

"Well, a long time ago the Everafter community decided that having giants running around Ferryport Landing was going to draw too much attention. Plus, giants are very unpredictable. They cause as much destruction when they're happy as they do when they're unhappy," Mrs. Grimm explained. "Once they get comfortable, it's impossible to move them, too. Imagine trying to plant seeds on your farm with a sleepy giant lying across it! So some folks came to our family and asked for help. Your great-uncle Edwin and your great-aunt Matilda dipped into our supply of magic beans—"

Sabrina coughed, hoping to get Daphne's attention, but the little girl shot her an angry look and turned back to the old woman.

"Edwin and Matilda planted a few and tricked the giants into climbing up the beanstalks. Once they were up in their home world, the cloud kingdom, Edwin and Matilda chopped the beanstalks down."

"What good did that do?" Daphne asked.

"Without giant beanstalks, there's no way for giants to come down here. Of course, not everyone was happy. In the old days, folks planted magic beans and climbed up the beanstalks just to steal the giants' treasures. It was dangerous, but if you were successful, you could make a fortune."

"Like Jack?" Daphne asked. "I know that story."

"You are correct, *liebling*. Jack robbed lots of giants and killed quite a number of them, too. In his day he was very rich and famous. They used to call him Jack the Giant Killer."

"Are you going to sit here and tell us that Jack was a real person?" Sabrina snapped.

"Now he works at a men's big-and-tall clothing shop on Main Street," Mr. Canis said.

"Granny, if all the beanstalks were destroyed, how did a giant get down here?" Daphne asked.

"Ah, *liebling*, that is the very mystery we are trying to solve," Mrs. Grimm said, taking out her notebook and flipping through her scribbles. "I believe someone planted a magic bean just to let a giant loose. We know his name is Englishman. We know he was going to videotape the giant. And we know he's got a bunch of goons working for him. There is one loose end, though. How did this Englishman get his hands on a magic bean? I was sure they were accounted for and locked safely away."

"And we have to figure out why this guy would want to let a giant loose in the first place," Daphne said. She jumped up and down in her seat like an excited puppy. It was obvious to Sabrina that her sister was falling in love with the old woman's stories.

"This is ridiculous," Sabrina grumbled.

Just then Elvis let out a low growl.

"Someone's coming," Mr. Canis warned as headlights flashed behind them.

"Everyone, get down," Mrs. Grimm urged.

They all squatted down and waited as a car passed by and parked on the side of the road. The old woman held her goggles to her eyes and studied it closely.

"Well, Sabrina, we've got more evidence for your theories. That's Mayor Charming's car," Mrs. Grimm said. "He and Mr. Seven are knocking on the cabin door."

Mr. Canis rolled his window down and sniffed the cool mountain air. His nose curled up as if he smelled something foul. Elvis had the same expression.

"Child, get the dog back into the car," Canis said to Sabrina.

"There's Tony. He's arguing with Charming about something," the old woman continued, still looking through her goggles. "Wait—there's someone else at the door."

"Get into the car, dog!" Mr. Canis shouted at Elvis. The Great Dane ignored him. He was busy sniffing the air and whining.

"Something's happening. Charming and Seven are running back to their car. Something has spooked them," Mrs. Grimm remarked. "And you won't believe who's with them!"

Sabrina braced herself. It was time to go. Canis was distracted by the dog, and the old woman was busy peering into her goggles. They wouldn't get a better chance. She grabbed her sister's hand and pulled Daphne out onto the road.

"What are you doing?" Daphne cried.

"We're getting out of here this minute!" Sabrina said.

Elvis let out another horrible whine. It was followed by an earthshaking thump that sent the girls tumbling to the ground.

"What was that?" Sabrina asked, trying to stand.

"Get into the car!" Mr. Canis ordered. His face was dark and serious.

"Forget it! We're not playing your crazy games any longer," Sabrina cried as she scrambled to her feet, then helped her sister do the same.

"Oh, dear! *Lieblings*, please, do as Mr. Canis says," Mrs. Grimm begged. "Something is coming."

"Something is coming? Is it a giant? Maybe it's the Tooth Fairy! The Easter Bunny? Do you really think we're that dumb? I don't want to hear another word about fairies and goblins and giants and Jack and the Beanstalk!" Sabrina raged as Elvis let out a shrieking howl. "I know the difference between reality and a fairy tale—"

Something fell out of the sky and stole the words out of her mouth. It was a monstrous hand that snatched the car off the ground. Sabrina couldn't believe what she was seeing, even though it was right there in front of her.

Her eyes traveled higher and higher. The hand led to a massive arm, then a bulging shoulder, and finally to an ill-shapen head. Boils as big as birthday cakes pocked its greasy skin. A broken nose zigzagged across its face, and one dead white eye seeped pus. Hairs as thick as tree trunks jutted out of the nostrils. It wore the hides of dozens of gigantic animals, including the head of what looked like a giant bear for a helmet. The dead bear's sharp fangs dug into the creature's bald scalp, threatening to pierce its brain. Its boots were made from hides, and tangled in the laces were several unfortunate saplings.

The giant lifted the family car up to its repugnant face and looked inside like a child inspecting a toy. With its free hand it picked its nose. "Where is Englishman?" it bellowed. "Why does he hide from me?"

The car was so high off the ground that Sabrina couldn't see what was going on inside it. The giant gave it a terrible shake, and she watched something fall out, landing with a *clang* at her feet. When she looked down she realized it was the old woman's handbag.

"You cannot hide from me, Englishman!" the giant shouted

as it lifted its enormous leg and stomped down hard on the little mountain cabin, flattening it like a pancake. Pieces of timber and stone flew into the air, missing the girls by inches. Sabrina and Daphne gasped. Had Tony, Steve, and Bobby managed to get out?

The giant let out a sickening laugh. It stuffed the car into a greasy shirt pocket, lifted its other humongous leg, and walked away, carrying the remains of the mountain cabin in the treads of its boots. The earth shook violently with each step, and ripples spilled across the land, like the disturbance a stone makes when it plunges into a pond. Because of its mammoth stride, the giant completely disappeared over the horizon in no time. Only the distant rumbling of its footfalls remained.

The girls stood completely frozen while Elvis howled and barked.

"She was telling the truth," Sabrina gasped.

"You were a snot to her the whole time, and now we might never see her again," Daphne cried, reaching down to scoop up Granny Relda's handbag, then she turned and marched down the road.

"Where are you going?"

"I'm going to rescue our family," the little girl called back without stopping.

5

ELVIS SNIFFED THE AIR WILDLY. SABRINA COULD see that he took his guard dog duties seriously. Every little buzz and cracking sound needed to be investigated. The dog darted back and forth, peering through the barbed-wire fence that separated the road from the endless forest. Once he was confident that the swaying limbs of the pines or the occasional rooting woodchuck was not a giant sneaking up on them, he trotted to the center of the road and put his huge nose back to work.

Sabrina, however, looked down the long empty road. They'd been walking for over an hour, and not so much as a bicycle had passed them. If they didn't get a ride back to the house soon, they would be walking all night.

The time might have passed more quickly if there was a little conversation, but for the last hour, Daphne had marched ahead of Sabrina, refusing to speak. Even Elvis, who followed closely behind, was ignoring her, but since he was a dog, his silence was a lot easier to bear.

"How was I supposed to know?" Sabrina cried. "Anybody would have thought she was crazy!"

"I didn't," Daphne said, finally breaking her silence.

"You don't count. You believe everything," Sabrina argued.

"And you don't believe anything," the little girl snapped. "Why are we even talking? You don't care what I think, anyway."

Sabrina wanted to defend herself, but she couldn't come up with words that rang true in her own mind. Daphne was right: What she thought hadn't mattered in a long, long time. But it wasn't like Sabrina wanted it that way. She was only eleven years old but was forced to act like an adult. It wasn't fun being the grown-up, constantly worrying about whether they were safe and fed and warm. Someone had to make the tough decisions, and unfortunately, she now realized, she had never considered what Daphne might want.

"Your opinion counts, OK?" Sabrina said. "The old woman—"

"Our grandma," Daphne corrected.

"Fine! Our *grandma* was just carried off by a giant. We're stuck in the middle of nowhere. I don't have a clue what to do next."

"You don't care if we ever find them," Daphne said. "Now you can run off like you planned with no one to stop you."

Daphne walked to a fallen tree trunk next to the road, sat

down, and began to cry. Elvis trotted over and nuzzled her, licking the little girl's tears from her chubby cheeks, and adding his whines to her sobbing.

Sabrina sat down beside them and put her arm around her sister. "Daphne, we're not running away. It's just . . . that monster was real. We can't fight that by ourselves. Even if we knew where it took them, I don't think we could get them back. What are a seven-year-old and an eleven-year-old going to do about a giant?"

"You're almost twelve," Daphne said, wiping her eyes on the sleeve of her fuzzy orange sweatshirt. "Besides, you heard Granny Relda. We're Grimms, and this is what we do. We take care of fairy-tale problems. We'll find a way to save Granny and Mr. Canis."

"How?"

"With this," Daphne said, holding the old woman's handbag above her head.

Sabrina took it from her sister and fumbled through it. Inside were the key ring, the piece of fabric the old woman had claimed came from a giant, a few heavy books, a notepad, and a small photograph. She pulled the last item out.

"Mom and Dad," she said as surprise raced through her. It was a picture of their parents, young and in love. Their dad's hand was on their mother's very pregnant belly, and they were both grinning. Granny Relda stood next to them, beaming; a stocky blond-haired man had his arm wrapped around her waist. Mr. Canis stood off to the side, as stone-faced as ever.

Sabrina held the snapshot as if it were a precious treasure. It was proof that her family existed, that she belonged somewhere. She could see her father's round face mirrored in his mother, and his sunflower-blond hair was a copy of his father's. Daphne had her mother's jet-black hair; Sabrina had her high cheekbones and bright eyes. They were all made from the same recipe.

Daphne hovered over her sister to get a better look, tears still running down her cheeks. Sabrina turned the picture over. Someone had written, *The Family Grimm—Relda, Basil, Henry, Veronica, Mr. Canis, and soon-to-be-born baby Sabrina.*

"Why did he lie to us?" Sabrina whispered as she tucked the family portrait safely into her pants pocket.

"He was trying to protect us," Daphne answered quietly.

"And what happens if we start to love Granny and she abandons us, too?" the older girl asked, trying to hide the hurt in her voice.

"Maybe she won't," Daphne said. "Maybe she'll just love us back."

"If we ever see her again."

The little girl wiped her eyes and dug into Granny Relda's handbag. She pulled out their grandmother's giant key ring.

"She threw this bag out of the car to us. She wants us to have these keys. There has to be something in the house that can help us rescue them."

If we can even get home, Sabrina said to herself as a light caught the corner of her eye. She looked down the road. There were headlights approaching. The two girls got up from the log and brushed themselves off.

"What should we do—stick out our thumbs?" Daphne asked.

Sabrina didn't know. They'd never hitchhiked before. In the past, whenever the girls had found themselves alone or on the run, they'd slipped under the turnstiles in the subway stations and traveled New York City's subterranean highway. This was new to Sabrina. She stuck out her thumb, and Daphne did the same. The car came to a screeching stop. It sat still for a moment, its engine humming, blinding the girls with its high-beam lights so that they had to shield their eyes with their hands.

"Well, that was easy," Daphne said. "What's he doing?"

Suddenly the car let out a long, eardrum-rattling honk, followed by more engine revving. To Sabrina, it seemed as if the car were an animal, waiting for the right time to pounce on them. She recalled hearing stories about hitchhikers being killed by lunatics. Hitchhiking didn't seem like such a great idea anymore. She grabbed her sister's hand and pulled her off the road. As if in response, the car revved its engine again, and the sound of squealing tires on asphalt filled the air.

"Run!" Sabrina cried. The two of them raced back the way they had come, hand in hand. Elvis followed closely behind, turning his big head to bark angry warnings at the menacing car, but this had no effect on whoever was behind the wheel. The car veered to the other side of the road, sped up, and passed the girls, then spun around, leaving black stains on the asphalt and the smell of burning rubber in Sabrina's nose. When it came to an abrupt stop, she realized it was a police car.

The door opened, and a short, pear-shaped man stepped out. He wore a beige police uniform with shiny black boots, a billy club that hung from his utility belt, and a wide-brimmed hat fastened under his three chins. His face was puffy and pink, with a nose that angled slightly upward, so that a person could see up his nostrils. On his shirt was a shiny metal star that read: FERRYPORT LANDING POLICE DEPARMENT. A name tag underneath it read: SHERIFF ERNEST HAMSTEAD.

"Girls, why are you running?" the sheriff asked in an unusually high-pitched voice that made Sabrina shiver.

"We thought you were trying to kill us," Daphne said angrily.

Sabrina flashed her a look, letting her know that she would do the talking.

"I'm sorry if I gave you two a start, but it's not safe for little girls like yourselves to be walking out here in the dark. These roads can be treacherous," the sheriff said.

"Treacherous?" Daphne asked.

"Dangerous," Sabrina explained.

"I got a call that you were out here, so I came looking," the portly man continued as he hoisted his sinking pants up around his waist. "Why don't you two hop into the squad car and I'll take you home?" He pointed to Elvis. "I don't know if we have room for your horse in there, but we'll try."

"He's not a horse," Daphne said. Then, realizing the sheriff was joking, she added, "You can't tease him. He's very sensitive."

Hamstead leaned down and scratched Elvis under the chin. "Oh, I'm sure he is, aren't you, Elvis?" The big dog growled and snapped at the sheriff's hand. Hamstead pulled it away just in time.

"How do you know Elvis?" Sabrina said suspiciously.

"Oh, Elvis and I have met many times. You must be Relda Grimm's grandchildren. I heard you were in town," he said. "I'm the local sheriff, Ernest Hamstead."

"I'm Daphne," the little girl offered.

"Sabrina," Sabrina muttered, still not sure she could trust him.

"So hop in, unless the two of you want to walk. It's a long way, though. Are you trying to raise a million dollars for the March of Dimes?" Hamstead opened the squad car's back door, and Elvis clumsily climbed inside. Sabrina and Daphne walked around the car and got in the front seat.

Sheriff Hamstead squeezed and shifted until he was behind the wheel, breathing heavily as if carrying a great burden. As soon as he was settled, he started up the squad car and drove in the direction of Granny's house.

"So I assume you two have already concocted a plan?" Hamstead asked.

The girls looked at each other, unsure of what to say.

"A plan?" Sabrina said, trying to play dumb.

"Yes. How are you going to rescue your grandmother and Mr. Canis?"

"You know about that?" Sabrina asked, dumbfounded.

Sheriff Hamstead shrugged. "Hard to miss a two-hundred-foot giant carrying grandmas away into the night, don't you think? I don't want you two girls to worry. Your granny is a tough cracker. I've seen her in bigger jams than this one, and besides, she's got the entire Ferryport Landing Police Department working on the case. I know you two have been trained for this kind of thing, but we like to take care of our own problems here in Ferryport Landing."

Daphne cupped her hand around Sabrina's ear. "Have we been trained?" she whispered.

"I don't know what he's talking about," Sabrina whispered back.

"Are you an Everafter?" the little girl said, returning her attention to the sheriff.

The sheriff looked over and winked a yes at Daphne. She squealed in delight.

"Which one?"

Suddenly the squad car's two-way radio crackled to life. "Hamstead? Sheriff Hamstead?" a man's voice fumed. It sounded oddly familiar to Sabrina.

The sheriff nervously grabbed at the handset. His sweaty hand fumbled it before he finally got hold of it.

"I'm here, boss. En route now," Hamstead said.

"That's fantastic news, Hamstead. Nice to know you can do something that's asked of you. As for our other problem, our little troublemaker has been arrested, and he's sitting in a cell as we speak."

"Good news, sir," Hamstead said.

"I'm *so* glad you approve," the man said. "Now get those little trolls back to the mansion, ASAP! I can't have any more headaches ruining tomorrow's festivities."

Sabrina's throat tightened with fear. When she looked at her sister, she saw the same horror reflected in Daphne's eyes. The voice on the police radio belonged to Mayor Charming!

"Daphne, do you remember that time Mr. and Mrs. Donovan took us to the three-day lima bean cook-off festival?" Sabrina asked casually, hoping the girl would remember the crazy foster couple they'd lived with for two weeks the previous year. The little girl's grimace told her the memory was still fresh and revolting. Mrs. Donovan was so proud of her pickled lima bean casserole, and the girls had been forced to act as taste testers. What Sabrina hoped was that Daphne also remembered their daring escape. Sabrina slipped her hand into her sister's, and when the car slowed to stop at a red light she quickly pulled on the door handle. Before Hamstead could react, the girls were out of the car and freeing Elvis from the backseat.

"Hey!"

The sisters ran to the side of the road where a five-foot barbed-wire fence lined the edge of the forest. There was no way to climb it; the fence's sharp teeth would tear them apart. Their only chance was to try to squeeze between the rusty wires to the other side. Desperately, Sabrina stood on one wire, then reached up and grabbed a safe spot on the next highest one. She pulled it upward with all her strength, creating a hole just big enough for her sister to crawl through.

"Go!" she shouted, carefully watching the portly sheriff struggling out of his car.

Daphne scurried through the gap, got to her feet, and tried to mimic the trick for her sister. The result was a space Sabrina couldn't possibly squeeze through.

"It's heavy," Sabrina coached Daphne. "You have to be strong."

"I'm trying!" the little girl cried, pulling harder.

"Girls! Get back into the car," Hamstead shouted angrily as he finally freed himself. He charged forward, but Elvis positioned his humongous body between the girls and the sheriff and growled until the man froze in his steps.

"Hurry," Daphne begged. "I can't hold it much longer!"

Sabrina got down on her hands and knees and tried to shimmy through the opening. She was nearly halfway through when Hamstead, dodging Elvis, grabbed her legs.

"You're coming with me!" he grunted as he tried to pull her back.

Sabrina kicked wildly, landing a couple painful blows to the man's chest and belly. He squealed in protest, making noises Sabrina had never heard come from a human being. When she looked back into the sheriff's face, what she saw bewildered her. Sheriff Hamstead was going through a disturbing metamorphosis. His pug nose became a slimy pink snout. His round face puffed up to three times its size, and his ears turned pointy and migrated to the top of his head. His chubby fingers melded into thick black hoofs, and his back bent over until he was literally on all fours. Hamstead turned into a pig—an angry, determined pig in a policeman's uniform.

Sabrina kicked once more and felt her foot sink into the pig's gelatinous belly. His face turned white, and he fell onto his back, honking and gasping for air as his little legs flailed back and forth. Just as suddenly, he changed back into a man and struggled to his feet.

Just then, Daphne's arms gave out and the barbed wire came down on top of Sabrina, snagging her pants. Daphne tried to lift it again, but the taut wire barely moved. Sabrina was trapped!

"Daphne, just go without me!" Sabrina cried, but the little girl shook her head in refusal. Suddenly she heard a series of notes, as if someone in the woods was playing a flute, followed by a buzzing sound that grew louder and louder. She peered through the trees nervously, remembering the music from the night before.

"They're coming, aren't they?" Daphne asked, just as a swarm of little lights zipped out of the forest and surrounded them. This time the lights didn't attack. Instead, they hovered above them, as if waiting for instructions. A single note pierced the night air, and the lights zipped into action, perching on the barbed wires that bit into Sabrina's pants, and with a flutter of tiny wings, pushed at the lowest wire, creating a hole big enough for Sabrina to crawl through. Sabrina wasn't sure if she could trust the flying menaces, especially after her last encounter, but Hamstead was marching toward her, so she freed herself from the top wire and crawled through as quickly as she could. The lights didn't release the fence until she was safely on the other side.

Hamstead stomped his foot in frustration, then ran up and down the length of the fence, searching for an opening big enough for his body. Desperately, he got onto his hands and knees and tried to squeeze through an impossibly small hole. That's when

Elvis made his move. The big dog—a runaway fur-covered train—ran full steam right at Hamstead and leaped onto the sheriff's broad back. Using it as a springboard, the dog sailed effortlessly to the other side of the fence.

The chubby policeman let out an "Oof!" but quickly recovered. He stood up, grabbed a fence post, and began to climb, rung by rung. Sabrina knew she had to act quickly. She grabbed another post, and, discovering it was quite loose in the ground, she shook it back and forth as hard as she could. The fence swayed uncontrollably, and the sheriff swayed with it.

"Hey, stop that!" Hamstead shouted nervously as he clung to the post.

Daphne rushed to Sabrina's side, and together they shook the fence even harder. Suddenly, with a loud tearing of fabric, Sheriff Hamstead thumped to the ground on his side of the fence. He groaned and let out an angry cry. After a moment he picked himself up, only to discover his pants had not survived the fall. They hung from the barbed wire's sharp teeth, leaving the sheriff in only a pair of droopy long johns. Defeated, he hobbled back to his car.

"He turned into a pig," Daphne whispered, still shaken from the experience.

"I saw him," Sabrina replied, then gestured behind them. "But I think we have another problem."

The little lights waited patiently nearby. They darted into the woods and then came back out, as if they wanted the girls to follow them.

"What do you want?" Sabrina asked, feeling slightly foolish for talking to insects, even after they shimmered and blinked an answer.

"I think they want us to follow them," said Daphne.

"I don't see that we've got much of a choice," Sabrina said, knowing the lights might attack if they didn't.

She took her sister's hand, and they walked into the dark woods with Elvis trotting closely behind. Low-hanging branches blocked their path, and each step required the girls to dodge and weave to get through. Several times Sabrina walked right into trees. But the lights patiently guided them, always slowing down to let them catch up.

Soon the girls stepped into a clearing. In the center was a pile of junk, not nearly as large as the one on Applebee's farm, and arranged in the shape of a massive chair. Sitting on this junk "throne" was a boy. He had a mop of blond hair that was tousled and dirty. He wore a pair of baggy blue jeans and a green hooded sweatshirt in desperate need of a washing. He held a small wooden sword in one hand, and perched on his head was a golden crown.

"Minions," he called to the little lights, "what have you found?"

The pixies erupted into loud buzzing.

HANG IN
THERE

"Spies, you say?" the boy asked. "Well, what do we do with spies?"

There was more buzzing in response, and a wicked grin stretched across the boy's dirty face.

"That's correct." He laughed. "We drown them!"

6

THE SWARM SURROUNDED THE GIRLS, DELIVERING several nasty stings and forcing them toward the boy, who had hopped down from his throne and was now guiding them all deeper into the forest.

"Where are you taking us?" Sabrina asked, but he just laughed.

Soon they came to the edge of the forest, where a tall fence blocked their way. Built into the fence was a gate, and the boy pushed it open. The girls stepped through and found themselves in front of a tarp-covered swimming pool in the backyard of a two-story suburban-style house. Some of the lights swirled around the tarp and lifted it off the pool, while others zipped off and returned with a rope. They stung Sabrina's arms relentlessly until she put them behind her back, and then they tied her wrists together.

The boy stuck the tip of his sword into Sabrina's back and forced her onto the diving board. "You've made a terrible mistake, spy!" he shouted.

"We're not spies!" Daphne exclaimed.

"Tell it to the fish!" the boy hollered, causing the pixies to make a tittering noise that sounded like laughter. Sabrina looked down into the pool and wondered how deep the water might be. There was a diving board, so she guessed it was deep, and with her arms tied behind her back she'd certainly drown if the icy water didn't freeze her to death first. She had to get free. She tugged at her wrists, but each pull just tightened the rope.

"So, spy, would you like to repent your crimes before you meet your watery doom?" the boy asked.

"What crimes?" Sabrina cried, and then took a deep breath, certain he would push her in. But after several moments, nothing happened.

"The crime of trying to steal the old lady away from me," the mop-topped boy declared.

"Granny?" Daphne asked.

"The one they call Relda Grimm."

"Relda Grimm is our grandmother, and we're not trying to steal her. We're trying to save her!" Sabrina shouted.

"Save her?" the boy asked suspiciously. "Save her from what?"

"A giant!" the two girls called out together.

Sabrina could sense their captor's confusion. She turned her head and saw him talking to several of the pixies that hovered nearby.

"Well, of course it makes a difference," the boy replied, annoyed.

"We're trying to get home. We need to save her before it's too late," Daphne pleaded.

The boy groaned and shook his head in disgust at the pixies. He reluctantly began to untie Sabrina's wrists.

"Where did this happen?" he asked as he worked. "How big was the giant?"

Sabrina didn't answer. Instead, as soon as she was free she spun around, grabbed the boy by the shoulders, and heaved him into the pool, sending a splash of water and soggy dead leaves high into the air. The sword slipped from his hand as he fell, and with nimble fingers, Sabrina caught it. She leaped to safety and waved the sword threateningly at the pixies.

"You're going to let us go," she demanded. There was no movement at first, but then the pixies flew around the pool, making the same laughing sound as before, as if they were chuckling at their leader's misfortune.

The girls stood dumbfounded, unsure of what to do next, when a geyser of water shot high into the air, with the thoroughly soaked boy riding its crest. When the water crashed back into the pool, the boy stayed aloft, held there by the powerful beating of the two huge wings on his back. Oddly enough, the boy was laughing.

"You think this is funny?" Sabrina exploded. She jabbed at the boy with his own sword, but he flew effortlessly away from each thrust. "You and your flying cockroaches kidnap girls and threaten to kill them? That's how you losers have fun?"

"Aww, we wouldn't have killed you. We were just fooling," the boy said.

"It was mean," Daphne said.

The boy shrugged. "Some people can't take a joke."

"Well, if you're finished with your stupid, psychotic games, my sister and I have to rescue our grandmother," Sabrina declared. She took Daphne's hand and turned to leave. Elvis joined them, but Sabrina shot him an angry look. The dog had spent the entire episode sitting lazily by the pool as if nothing peculiar were happening. The Great Dane caught her eye and whined.

"You've been in this town for less than two days, and you've already lost the old lady," the boy said bitterly as he floated down into their path.

"We didn't *lose* her," Sabrina replied. "She was taken by a monster as big as a mountain."

"Well, if you've come looking for help, you're talking to the wrong person," the boy declared. "Rescuing old ladies is a job for a hero. I'm a villain."

"Good to know! We weren't going to ask anyway!" Sabrina said angrily, tossing the boy's sword aside.

"I thought that Peter Pan was one of the good guys," Daphne added.

The boy's face turned so red Sabrina thought his head might explode. "Peter Pan? I'm not Peter Pan! I'm Puck!"

"Who's Puck?" Daphne asked.

"*Who's Puck*?" the boy cried. "I'm the most famous Everafter in this town. My exploits are known around the world!"

"I've never heard of you," Sabrina said. She spun around and started walking through the yard to the road, with her sister and Elvis following. After only a couple of steps, the boy was hovering in front of them again.

"You've never heard of the Trickster King?" Puck asked, shocked. The girls shook their heads. "The Prince of Fairies? Robin Goodfellow? The Imp?"

"Do you work for Santa?" Daphne asked.

"I'm a fairy, not an elf!" Puck roared. "You really don't know who I am! Doesn't anyone read the classics anymore? Dozens of writers have warned the world about me. I'm in the most famous of all of William Shakespeare's plays."

"I don't remember any Puck in *Romeo and Juliet*," Sabrina muttered, feeling a little amused at how the boy was reacting to his non-celebrity.

"Besides *Romeo and Juliet*!" Puck shouted. "I'm the star of *A Midsummer Night's Dream*!"

"Congratulations," Sabrina said flatly. "Never read it."

Puck floated down to the ground. His wings disappeared, and he spun around on his heel, transforming into a big shaggy dog. Elvis growled at the sight of him, but Puck didn't attack. Instead, he shook himself all over, spraying the girls with water. When he was finished, he morphed back into a boy.

"The old lady is a goner!" Puck taunted. "You'll get no help from me. Like I said, I'm a bad guy."

"Yeah, you told us," Sabrina said as she wiped her face.

"I really can't help," he said.

"Fine!"

"Fine!"

"You sent those pixies to attack us last night, didn't you? That wasn't very nice." Daphne gave him her best angry look.

"I'm a lot of things, but nice isn't one of them," the boy said.

The girls turned their backs on Puck and marched off down the road. When they were out of his earshot, Daphne tugged on Sabrina's arm.

"Maybe we should team up with him? He could fly over the forest and spot the giant," she suggested.

"You saw what a lunatic he is. I don't want him to ruin whatever slim chance we might have," Sabrina replied. "We're better off on our own."

The path to the front door of Granny Relda's cottage seemed like a walk up a mountain, and by the time they arrived at the house Sabrina was nearly asleep standing up. She took out Granny's key ring and felt the weight of a hundred keys jingling in her hand, each singing a different mystery. There were a lot of locks on the front door, but not enough for each of these keys. Where were the doors the rest of them unlocked?

It seemed like hours before Sabrina finally turned the last dead bolt on the door. Elvis was asleep and drooling on the path, his thick legs kicking back and forth as he dreamed. Daphne lay beside him, using his big belly as a pillow.

"That's all of them." She twisted the knob and leaned into the door. Unfortunately, it didn't swing open. In fact, it didn't budge at all. "It's jammed."

Daphne got up and walked over. "Are you sure you unlocked them all?" she asked.

Sabrina fumed. If she knew anything, it was how to unlock a door. They'd escaped from a dozen foster homes in the last year and a half. Locks were not her problem. She took the cold doorknob in her hand and turned it once more, proving that she had unlocked it.

"You're going to save the old lady from a giant? You can't even open a door," a familiar voice commented. Puck floated to the ground, his huge wings disappearing just as he landed.

"What do you want?" Sabrina demanded.

"If you want to get inside, you have to tell the house you're home," he said.

"Of course!" Daphne knocked on the door three times. "We're home," she said, repeating the same words the girls heard Granny Relda say each time they entered the house, while turning the doorknob. The door finally swung open.

"How did you know that?" Daphne asked Puck.

"The old lady and I are close. She tells me everything."

Elvis immediately leaped to his feet and trotted into the house, nearly knocking over the girls on his way to the kitchen. Sabrina and Daphne stepped inside, but when Puck pushed his way in they tried to close the door in his face.

"We're not supposed to let anyone in here," Sabrina said, suddenly thankful for Granny's odd rules.

Puck spun around, morphed into a mouse, and skittered into the room before they could stop him. A moment later he was back to his normal form and tossing himself onto Granny's fluffy recliner.

"Now, I know I'm one of the bad guys, so you two will have to keep this to yourselves," the boy said. "I do have a reputation as the worst of the worst. If word got out that the Trickster King was helping the heroes . . . well, it would be scandalous. But the old lady does provide me with a meal from time to time. Not that

I feel any loyalty, but if she were to get eaten by a giant, my free lunches would disappear. So I did a flyby, all the way up into the mountains. I found some tracks, but no giant. I sent some pixies to keep searching without me. The whole thing was exhausting. The two of you should get started."

"Started doing what?" Sabrina cried.

"First, I want you two to prepare me a hearty meal so that I have plenty of energy to kill the giant," Puck instructed the girls.

Sabrina groaned. "You've got to be kidding."

"The old lady always makes lunch when a mystery is afoot. I know it's not the most glamorous work, but I think you two are best suited for domestic tasks."

"What does 'domestic tasks' mean?" Daphne asked.

The girls stared at Puck, waiting for an answer.

"You know—women's work," he said, only to be shouted down by the angry sisters. "Well, I can't be expected to do everything. Being your leader is going to take all of my energy."

"Leader! No one made you leader. No one even said they wanted your help!"

"You may not want it, but you need it," the boy shouted back. "The two of you can't even get into your own house. Do you think you'll strike fear into a giant?"

"Maybe if you two keep shouting, the giant will come to us," Daphne said.

Sabrina and Puck stared angrily at each other for a long moment.

"Who's hungry?" Daphne said. "I'm going to go do some domestic tasks for myself."

Sabrina was too hungry to fight any longer. Eating would clear her head.

The three children raided the refrigerator and dug through the breadbox, grabbing anything and everything they could get their hands on. Puck seemed to share Daphne's big appetite; both of their plates were heaped with odd-colored food. The two also ate the same way—like hungry pigs, grunting happily as they gobbled up their meals. They were working on seconds by the time Sabrina finished making a Swiss cheese sandwich and found what she hoped was just a weirdly colored pear.

"So what's with the hat?" Daphne asked, pointing to Puck's golden crown.

"It's a crown," Puck huffed. "I'm the Prince of Fairies; Emperor of Pixies, Brownies, Hobgoblins, Elves, and Gnomes; King of Tricksters and Prank-Players; spiritual leader to juvenile delinquents, layabouts, and bad apples."

The little girl stared at the boy with confusion in her face.

"I'm royalty!" Puck declared.

"So where's your kingdom?" Sabrina asked snidely.

"You're in it!" he snapped. "The forest and the trees are my kingdom. I sleep under the stars. The sky is my royal blanket."

"That explains the smell," Sabrina muttered.

The Trickster King ignored her comment and munched hungrily, tossing apple cores and whatever else he couldn't eat onto the floor. A turkey bone soared from his hand and landed on a nearby windowsill.

"Puck, can I ask you a question?" Daphne said.

"You bet."

"If you knew Shakespeare, why do you look like you're only eleven years old?"

This was something Sabrina wondered as well. Granny's explanation that magic kept the Everafters alive didn't totally make sense. If Mayor Charming and Mr. Seven were the same people from the stories, they had to be hundreds of years old, yet they looked as if they were no older than her dad.

"Ah, that's the upside of being an Everafter," Puck said. "You only get as old as you want to be. Some decided to age a little so that they could get jobs and dumb stuff like that."

"Then why didn't you?" Sabrina asked.

Puck shrugged. "Never crossed my mind. I plan on staying a boy until the sun burns out."

Sabrina thought that she'd like to see him running around in the dark as the earth froze over. She bit into her sandwich, only to discover that the Swiss cheese tasted more like hard applesauce.

"So, tell me what happened with the giant," said Puck. While

Sabrina ate, Daphne told the boy the whole sordid story. She told him about the crushed farmhouse that was stepped on by a giant's foot and how Mayor Charming demanded that Granny Relda give up her detective work. How the farmer spoke to a man named Mr. Englishman, and how a witch erased his memory of the entire event. She told about the gang of thugs that attacked them outside the hospital, and how, when they followed the gang back to their hideout, they spotted Charming again. Then she told him about the giant's attack, and how he snatched up Granny and Mr. Canis.

While Daphne told the story, Sabrina wandered into the living room and stood in front of one of the many bookshelves.

"Books on giants . . . where would they be?" she said to herself.

Puck and Daphne eventually joined her, and together they scanned the bookcases.

"There's got to be something here that can help with that monster," Sabrina said after many minutes of searching.

"Look!" Daphne said, pointing at a row of old books.

Instead of guides to giants, Sabrina saw their family name repeated in each title. She took one down and read the whole title: *Fairy-Tale Accounts, 1942–1965, by Edwin Alvin Grimm.*

"It's a journal," Sabrina said, flipping through it to find pages and pages of handwritten notes, going back decades.

"There's one here for everyone in our family, I guess—including this one," said Daphne as she pulled another one from the shelf and handed it to her sister. Sabrina almost dropped it when she saw the title: *Fairy-Tale Accounts by Henry Grimm*. She opened it and recognized her dad's neat handwriting right away. She traced his hand's movement along the lines and circles of each word. She turned more pages, feeling more of his presence—not bothering to read, just taking comfort in knowing that he had once held the book.

"Let me see," Daphne said.

"You're wasting your time with these stupid books. I'm the smartest person I know, and I've never read a book in my life. We should all be out looking," Puck said.

"If you want to go, there's nothing keeping you here," Sabrina said as she led her sister back into the kitchen. She laid the journal down on the table, and the two girls hovered over it together. They flipped to the first page. A color photograph of Mayor Charming, dressed in royal robes, stared back at them. He wore a sapphire-and-diamond crown, and a dazzling ruby ring on each finger. He smiled smugly, as if he thought very highly of himself.

Elvis sauntered into the room and licked Sabrina's hand. He spied Charming's picture and growled.

"Don't worry, Elvis! He can't get us now," Daphne said.

Sabrina read aloud what her father had written:

"July—Another run-in with Charming. Mom and Dad discovered that he was attempting to buy a thousand acres of land known as Old McDonald's Farm on the eastern border of the town. Where he got the money for such a big purchase came into question, and Dad, of course, accused him of using his witches to conjure up phony cash. Charming huffed and demanded an apology. When Dad refused, the two of them got into a fistfight (Dad has one heck of a left hook! KA-POW!). But the biggest surprise was Charming's freak-out. He swore he'd turn Ferryport Landing into his new kingdom, and he said he looked forward to the day when he could personally drive a bulldozer through our house.

"He's rebuilding his kingdom," Sabrina said as she turned the pages. "It's all in here. Listen to this:

"December—Charming lost the most when he moved to America. He was forced to sell his castle, his horses, everything he owned. To make it worse, one of the three ships Wilhelm hired for the Atlantic crossing was used primarily to haul Charming's enormous fortune, and it sank when it hit a sandbar off the coast of Maryland. When he got to Ferryport Landing (changed from Fairyport Landing in 1910), he blew what was left on one bad investment after another: a failed diamond mine partnership with the dwarfs; a wholesale carpet company poorly managed by his business partner, Ali Baba; and a laser

disc player factory that went belly-up. Being mayor doesn't pay much, and Dad believes Charming runs a bunch of financial scams—both illegal and magical—just to keep the electricity on at the mansion. That was until he came up with his greatest scheme yet: the Ferryport Landing Fund-raising Ball. Once a year, Charming invites the Ever-after community to the mansion, and every year they throw money at him, trying to win his support for whatever political cause they have. The money obviously goes straight into the prince's pocket. I'd bet anything that Charming is hoarding most of it so he can buy up the whole town."

"But what's that got to do with giants? And if he wanted to buy the farm, why did he send that Mr. Englishman to do the work?" Daphne asked.

"I believe that Mr. Englishman and Mayor Charming are the same person. Charming does have an English accent. He could have worn a disguise so Mr. Applebee wouldn't recognize him as the mayor," Sabrina said.

"I bet you're right!" her sister said. "But still, why let a giant loose? I don't get it."

"In the old days, giants and people used to work together all the time," Puck said, stealing the purple pear from Sabrina's plate and chomping on it.

"They did?"

"Oh yeah. Folks used to hire them to take care of problems they couldn't handle themselves. From what I hear you can pretty much talk them into doing anything," the boy said. "Giants are pretty dumb."

"He's right." Daphne was poring over a large book she'd come across while Sabrina was reading. It was entitled *Anatomy of a Giant*. "I don't know what this word is," she said.

"How is it spelled?"

"A-L-L-I-A-N-C-E-S."

"It's *alliances*; it means to team up or join a group," Sabrina explained.

"It says that in olden days people used to form all-all . . ."

"Alliances."

". . . alliances with giants to destroy their enemies."

"Charming's using the giant to scare people off their land. Anyone who won't sell gets squashed!" Sabrina cried.

"But why have Glinda erase Mr. Applebee's mind?" Daphne asked.

"What do you mean?"

"Why would he want the farmer to forget to be afraid? And don't forget the lens cap," Daphne said. "Why would he want to videotape it?"

"You're right. It doesn't make sense. I don't think I'd want any proof of what I'd done if it were me," Sabrina said.

"There's more," her sister said, looking down at the big book. "It also says that rarely did these all-all . . ."

"Alliances."

"Yeah, it says they usually backfired. In most cases, the human was eaten by the giant or dragged off to the giant kingdom to be a slave. There's a story here about a giant kidnapping a princess for an evil baron, and before the baron could collect a ransom from her family, the giant ate her," Daphne said quietly.

"That's hilarious!" Puck said.

Sabrina and Daphne gave him a disgusted look.

"It says the townspeople used hound dogs to track down the giant because giants have a strong smell," Daphne continued. "When they caught him, he nearly killed the entire town before they could bring him down."

The girls spent a moment looking into each other's worried eyes. What if the giant had eaten Granny and Mr. Canis? What if he was eating them as they wasted time doing research?

"It says when giants got out of hand, the townspeople sent a hero to kill the giant for them," Daphne read. "His name was Jack, and in his prime, he killed between ten and twenty giants, stole treasure from the giant kingdom, and was world-famous."

Sabrina turned her attention back to her father's journal. She flipped through more of its pages until she found an envelope stuffed inside.

"Look at this!" she said. "It says, *To Sabrina, Daphne, and Puck. From Granny Relda.*"

"See! I told you I knew her!" Puck cried.

"Open it," Daphne begged.

Sabrina tore open the envelope and began to read the letter inside.

"Lieblings, if you're reading this, then one of my investigations has not turned out the way I hoped. I don't want you to worry, as I can take care of myself, and I know a little kung fu. If for some reason there is an emergency, you should take my keys and go to the room you have been forbidden to enter. All the answers you need will be staring you in the face.

Love,

Your oma

P.S. Don't give Elvis any sausage. It makes him gassy."

"She wants us to go into the room?" Puck said in amazement. "I've been trying to get in there since the day she told me it was off-limits!"

"Staring us in the face? What does that mean?" Sabrina said, but before she knew it, her little sister was halfway up the stairs with the key ring in her hand.

"Wait!" Sabrina shouted, taking the stairs two at a time. By the time she got to the top, Daphne was already trying keys.

Puck flew up the stairs and snatched the ring out of Daphne's hands.

"Royalty first, peasant."

"She gave these keys to *us,*" Sabrina snapped, snatching them from him.

"A set of keys you have no idea how to use!" Puck shouted, taking them back.

"Hand them over, stinky!" shouted Sabrina.

"No!"

"Don't make me do something you're going to regret."

"I've fought tougher guys than you, Grimm. Though most of them had better-smelling breath!"

"KNOCK OFF THAT RACKET RIGHT NOW!" a voice suddenly boomed from behind the door.

It startled them all so much that they fell backward onto the floor.

"Did you hear that?" Daphne whispered.

"Everyone heard that," Sabrina and Puck replied.

"Maybe it's the sheriff? Maybe he got into the house somehow?" Daphne said.

"Hamstead would have just come down and grabbed us," her sister replied. "Besides, Elvis isn't freaking out."

"Then who is it?" Puck asked.

"Granny locks this door for a reason. If there's someone in

that room, she doesn't want them going anywhere. They might be dangerous," Sabrina warned.

"I'm not afraid!" the boy cried, puffing up his chest.

"I have an idea," Daphne said. She took Puck's and Sabrina's hands and led them back down the stairs and into the kitchen.

Within minutes, the girls and Puck were standing outside the door again, each wearing a metal spaghetti strainer as a helmet. Daphne wore an ancient washing board on her chest and had duct-taped huge metal spoons to each kneecap as protection from unfair kicks. She held a frying pan as her weapon. Sabrina wore a pressure-cooker lid on her behind and held a wok pan for a shield. She swung a rolling pin in the air, preparing to whack whoever might be on the other side of the door. Puck held his trusty sword in one hand and a carrot peeler in the other. He'd found a couple of cookie pans to tape to his chest and back, and his feet were encased in oven mitts.

Sabrina bent down to insert what she thought was the right key, and her "armor" clanged and knocked around, causing a tremendous racket. She realized that a sneak attack was probably no longer realistic. When the key turned in the lock, she straightened up and looked back at the others.

Elvis stood behind Daphne and Puck with an odd, confused expression on his face.

"We should send the dog in first," Sabrina said.

"Good idea," Daphne replied.

Sabrina said to the Great Dane, "Elvis—go get him!"

Elvis sat down on his hind legs and used his back paw to scratch his neck. If he understood the order, he wasn't letting on. Discouraged, Sabrina said to her sister and Puck, "We'll go in together."

"Whoever is in there better leave, 'cause we're armed to the teeth. I wouldn't want to be you when we find you!" Puck shouted.

"Just stay together and, most of all, stay calm," Sabrina said. "If we don't panic, we can take this guy ourselves."

"On three," Daphne whispered, giving her frying pan a practice swing.

"ONE, TWO, THREE!" Sabrina screamed, shoving open the door and rushing into the room with the others at her back. The trio swung their weapons frantically, slashing at whatever enemy dared to face their deadly kitchen utensils. After several moments, and zero hits, Sabrina stopped and looked around the room. In the moonlight from the room's only window, she could see it was empty, except for a wood-framed, full-length mirror that hung on a wall.

"Where did he go?" Daphne said as she peered behind the door and found no one.

"He ran off, 'cause he's smart!" Puck crowed. "He knew we'd skin him alive."

Sabrina frowned. "Then we may have run off our only chance at saving Granny and Mr. Canis. There's nothing in here that's going to help us."

She turned to leave, but Daphne said, "Granny's note said that all the answers we need would stare us in the face." She pointed at the mirror.

"It's just a mirror," her sister argued.

"It can't hurt to take a look," Puck said, and trotted over to it.

Sabrina followed Daphne, and together they studied their reflections.

"I think I see something," Puck said.

"What? What is it?" Sabrina said.

"A booger. It's in your nose." The boy laughed so hard he snorted, but then he saw Sabrina staring and stopped abruptly.

"WHO ARE YOU?" a loud voice suddenly bellowed from within the mirror. Sabrina looked into it and felt the hairs on the back of her neck stand on end. A face was staring out at her, but it was not her own. Floating without a body, the face was that of a man with a bald head and thick, angular features. He stared at the children with rage, his eyes like blue flames. Terrified, the children ran back toward the exit, but a blue ray shot from the mirror, hit the door, and slammed it shut, trapping them inside.

"WHO ARE YOU?" the head bellowed. "TELL ME NOW OR I WILL KILL YOU WHERE YOU STAND!"

7

"I WILL ROAST THE FLESH FROM YOUR BONES!" the face threatened.

A six-foot-high circle of fire snaked around the group, trapping them within. The flames licked at the pots and pans the children wore as armor, scorching Sabrina's hand. She rubbed the painful burn.

Dark gray clouds framed the bulbous head in the mirror in a violent thunderstorm. Lightning crackled around the face, exploding in light and sound with every twitch of its eyebrows.

"Who dares to invade my sanctuary?"

Sabrina pulled Daphne close to her, while Puck stepped in front of them and thrust his little sword into the wall of fire. "We're not invaders! We live here!" he shouted.

The face cocked an eyebrow and looked at them sternly. "You're the grandchildren?"

"Yes! Sabrina and Daphne!" Sabrina shouted.

"And Puck!" Puck chimed in.

Suddenly the fire puttered out, as if someone had turned off a stove.

"Forgive me. I thought carnival folk were invading the house," the head declared. "You can hardly blame me, when three kids break into my room dressed like escaped inmates from the Ferryport Landing Asylum. You may not have heard, but the whole circus-clown-meets-crazy-street-vagrant look is so over."

Sabrina looked down at her outfit: the torn, bright blue pants, the orange sweatshirt with the monkey, the pressure-cooker lid strapped to her behind. Her face flushed with embarrassment as she took off her spaghetti-strainer helmet.

"What are you?" she asked, regaining her composure.

"I'm not a what—I'm a who!" the face in the mirror croaked, looking deeply insulted.

"Then *who* are you?"

"Tsk, tsk, tsk. Why, I'm the seer of seers . . . the visionary of visionaries . . . the man who puts the fun in your reflection," he replied with a dramatic flourish.

Sabrina looked at her sister for help. Daphne had read more fairy tales than Sabrina, but the little girl returned her sister's gaze with a dumbfounded shrug.

The face in the mirror frowned, sensing that the girls were far from starstruck and, in fact, had no idea who he was. "I'm the magic mirror!" he snapped.

"We could have guessed you were a magic mirror," Puck muttered.

"Not *a* magic mirror! *The* magic mirror! 'Mirror, mirror, on the wall'?"

"From 'Snow White'?" Daphne asked.

"Is there another?" the face growled. "You can call me Mirror. Your grandma told me you were coming from New York City, though she didn't tell me she was giving you a set of keys."

"She didn't. Granny threw hers to us before she was carried off by a giant," Daphne explained.

Mirror's eyes grew wide with astonishment. "Well, there's a sentence you don't hear every day. I suppose you are in the midst of a rescue plan?"

"*They* are," Puck said defensively. "I'm a villain."

"So, let's hear this thrilling plan," said Mirror.

"We haven't got all the details worked out yet," Sabrina said, trying to make herself sound older and more mature.

"You don't have a plan!" Mirror exclaimed.

"We're still working on it," Sabrina said defensively. "We thought there might be something up here that could help us."

"You're just like Henry." Mirror sighed. "Ready to jump headfirst into an adventure, hoping he'd come up with a plan along the way."

Sabrina was shocked. *Headfirst* didn't sound like her dad at all. *My dad read the labels on cans of food before everyone could eat*, she thought.

"You knew our father?" Daphne exclaimed.

"Knew him? I was Henry's babysitter most of the time. I saw him off to the prom. I was even invited to your parents' wedding. They propped me up on my own seat. I am a member of this family, after all."

"Sorry, we didn't mean to offend you," the little girl said. "So if you're the magic mirror, what do you do?"

"I can show you anything you want to see. All you have to do is ask," Mirror said proudly.

"What are you talking about?" Sabrina asked with growing impatience. All this chatter was keeping them from acting. Who knew what that monster was doing to Granny and Mr. Canis?

"You got a question, I got an answer," the face bragged. "All you have to do is ask."

"Are Granny Relda and Mr. Canis still alive?" Daphne asked.

"Sorry, kiddo, that's not how it works. You have to ask me the right way."

"What's the right way?" Sabrina demanded.

"Well, if you're going to be cranky, then just forget it!" Mirror said. He jutted out his lower lip.

Puck swung his carrot peeler menacingly at the face, then realized what he was doing and flashed his little sword. "Listen,

Mirror, you tell us what we want to know, or you're going to find yourself cracked and broken all over the floor!"

"You wouldn't dare!"

"Just see if I wouldn't!"

Daphne tugged on Puck's arm. Acting as the diplomat for the group, she apologized to Mirror and explained, "We're just very eager to find our granny and Mr. Canis, and we don't understand what you are saying."

The face's expression changed to a huge smile. "Apology accepted. Now, like I was going to say before I was so rudely interrupted," he said as he eyed Sabrina disapprovingly, "you have to ask your questions in a special way to activate the magic. You have to—"

"Rhyme them!" Daphne interrupted with a happy cry.

"Bingo!"

The little girl turned to the other two. "We have to rhyme the question. Like, 'Mirror, mirror, on the wall, who's the fairest of them all?'"

A blue mist filled the mirror's surface, and the face was replaced with the image of the most beautiful woman Sabrina had ever seen. She had gorgeous black hair like Daphne's, and flawless porcelain skin. She was standing in front of a classroom, teaching. Every boy in the class stared at her like a lovesick puppy, and there was a pile of apples on her desk.

"That would still be the lovely Snow White," Mirror said.

Just then, all the students got up from their seats and exited the room. When Snow White was finally alone, she tossed the apples into a garbage can and slid it under her desk.

"OK, how about this?" Sabrina said. "Mirror, mirror, in a beehive, is Granny Relda still alive?"

Mirror's face reappeared, and he was frowning. "In a beehive?"

"All you said was it had to rhyme. You didn't say it had to make sense."

"Very well," said the face, and the blue mist returned. "Your grandmother is alive and well, for now."

"Where is she?" Daphne asked.

"Uh-uh. One question at a time. And, anyway, that one didn't rhyme."

"Mirror, mirror, we're just kids, can you show us where our grandma is?" Puck asked.

"Sorry, that doesn't technically rhyme," Mirror argued.

"It's close enough!" the children shouted.

Mirror frowned but misted over; suddenly, Granny and Mr. Canis appeared in the reflection. They were climbing on top of their car, which was enclosed in what could only be described as a giant bag. Mr. Canis pulled the fabric down, and the two of them looked over the edge. They were still in the giant's shirt pocket.

"They're alive!" Daphne sighed with relief as the image zoomed out to show the giant. The ugly brute was asleep, lounging against a huge rocky outcropping.

"He's up in the mountains. Look at the size of that beast. I'm going to need a bigger sword," Puck said.

"We'll come with you," Daphne said.

"You aren't going anywhere," the boy replied. "The last thing I need is a couple of girls bawling while I fight the giant. You two are staying here."

"What are we supposed to do while that's happening?" Sabrina asked. "And so help me, if you say *women's work* again . . ."

"Oh no, you didn't," Mirror said to Puck, who grinned.

"If anyone's going up there, it's me!" Sabrina declared. "I can't trust some smelly kid who lives in the woods to save my grand-mother. You couldn't even push me into a pool. You stay here and keep an eye on Daphne!"

"*Keep an eye on Daphne*?" Daphne repeated indignantly. "I'm not staying here! She's my granny, too!"

"What you need is someone who has experience with giants," Mirror interrupted.

"Fine, let's find an expert. Mirror, mirror, what can we do, to rescue Granny from you know who?" Sabrina asked.

"Not bad!" The mirror misted over once again, and this time when it cleared the children saw a man in a jail cell. He had a boy-ish face with spiky blond hair and big eyes. He was lying lazily on a thin, ratty cot. He got up, walked over to a small window, looked out, pulled on the bars in a hopeless effort to free himself, and when he found them unbendable, scowled and returned to his dingy bed.

"You need the help of Jack the Giant Killer," Mirror said as his face returned to the reflection.

"That guy sitting in jail has killed giants? I'm not impressed," Puck said, sulking.

"Granny said he was down on his luck," Sabrina said. "But I didn't think she meant *that* down. I guess it'll be easy to find him now."

"We passed the jailhouse on the way to the hospital," her sister pointed out.

"We do not need Jack," Puck fumed. "I'm more than able to kill big ugly all by myself!"

Suddenly Elvis barked an angry warning from downstairs. It was followed by several loud knocks on the front door.

"Who's that?" Sabrina whispered.

"Mirror, mirror, one question more, who's that knocking on our door?" Daphne asked.

"Now you're getting the hang of it!" Mirror said as his face misted over. Outside of the house, two police cars were parked in the driveway. "It seems as if the local authorities have arrived."

"Hamstead's here," Sabrina said as the image revealed the fat sheriff hoisting up a new pair of pants in between angry knocks on the front door. An equally plump deputy with a thick handlebar mustache gestured for Hamstead to walk around the house, and together they did, revealing pink curly tails sticking out of the backs of their beige slacks.

"He's brought friends," Daphne said as the image blurred, then reappeared from another angle. Another equally rotund deputy with a shock of bright white hair tucked under his hat walked along the side of the house, trying to find an open window. When he got to the dining room window, he placed his face against it to peer in, only to fall over backward when Elvis lunged at him from the other side. The terrified deputy transformed into a pig, but changed back once he calmed down.

"Ferryport's finest, Deputies Swineheart and Boarman," said Mirror.

"I can't believe the Three Little Pigs are working for the bad guy." Daphne sighed.

"I can't believe anyone still calls them the three *little* pigs." Mirror tittered. "That trio has been tipping the scales for as long as I can remember."

"Girls—this is the police. Open the door," the sheriff demanded through a megaphone in a tinny, amplified voice.

"What do we do?" Daphne asked.

"We'll never get past them," Sabrina said.

"Sounds like the old lady is a goner. There go my hot lunches," Puck said with a sigh.

"What is this nonsense I'm hearing?" Mirror said. "You are Grimms. Performing the impossible is what you do. Do you think your family could have survived this long with ogres and monsters running around if they couldn't find a way out of their own house?"

"OK, you're so smart, you tell us what to do," Sabrina snapped. "Or do we have to rhyme to get your help?"

"Temper, temper, Sabrina. Ask, my little wardrobe-challenged friend, and you shall receive," the face said. "All I need is your keys."

"What? Why?" Sabrina asked.

"Do you want my help or not? Give me the keys." The reflection warped, and a portion of the mirror's surface grew outward, as if someone were blowing a bubble from the other side. It pushed out farther and farther, causing the reflection to shimmer and ripple until a hand was thrust through. Even Puck seemed unsettled by what he was seeing.

"C'mon, blondie, I don't have all night," Mirror snapped.

Sabrina put the keys on the hand, and it disappeared back into the bubble.

"I'll be right back," the face said as it vanished and the surface of the mirror flattened, returning to normal.

After several moments, the face reappeared. "I've got just the thing for you," Mirror said with a smile. Again, the surface of the glass rippled, and this time a dusty, rolled-up carpet came through. Once it completely broke the surface, the carpet fell to the ground, where it unrolled before them.

Dazzling burgundy and gold threads formed an intricate pattern of symbols: moons, stars, flowers, sickles, and triangles, which seemed to shimmer as if they were woven from precious metal. Golden roped tassels hung from the carpet's edges.

"What's this?" Daphne asked, stepping on the carpet. Suddenly it lifted off the floor and hovered in the air. The movement was so quick that Daphne fell onto her backside. "It flies!"

"Just a little thing your grandpa picked up during a trip to the Middle East. Maybe you've heard of Aladdin?" Mirror said proudly. "This is his flying carpet. Thought it might be the best thing for your little rescue mission. Just tell it where you want to go, and it'll get you there. Even if you don't know how to get there yourself."

"How do I make it go down?" Daphne asked, giggling, but no sooner had the question left her lips than the carpet fell to the ground, causing Daphne's "armor" to clang on the floor.

"When you're finished with it, I expect you to return it," said Mirror sternly as Granny's keys came back through the surface and fell to the ground. Sabrina picked them up.

"But how are we going to get out of the house?" Sabrina asked.

"Listen, cowgirl, I can't do it all for you. From what I hear, you're quite the expert at being sneaky. I suggest you cause a diversion," Mirror said.

"With what?"

Puck laughed to himself.

"What?" Sabrina asked the boy.

"Nothing. I just have a brilliant plan to get us out of this house, but it's something a hero would do. It's really not my style. Then again, it does call for some mischief. Oh well, you said you didn't want my help. I'll just step aside and let you two geniuses do your thing."

Sabrina groaned and tried her best to sound sweet. "Please, Puck, will you help us?"

Puck grinned. "I believe the words you are looking for are *Please, Your Majesty, leader of this big adventure, would you be so kind as to save my behind?*"

The girls carried the carpet down the stairs and into the kitchen, where they laid it on the floor. They removed their "armor," and Sabrina opened the refrigerator. Granny's odd and abundant cooking filled the shelves. It would take an army to eat it all. As Puck supervised, the girls pulled out pies, cakes, oddly colored fruits, and several things Sabrina couldn't identify, and tossed them onto the carpet. Elvis sat by, drooling with hunger, obviously wondering if the heap of food was for him.

"There's nothing a pig can resist less than a buffet," Puck said.

"Is this enough?" Daphne asked.

"I hope so," Puck answered. "Carpet, up!"

The carpet rose to waist height and hovered next to the children.

"Come!" Sabrina commanded, and the carpet followed them as they walked to the front door.

Daphne peeked out the window. "They're sitting on the hoods of their squad cars," she said. "Puck, are you ready?"

The boy took off the last of his kitchen armor and pulled a small flute from his sweatshirt pocket.

"You don't have to ask the Trickster King if he is ready," he said arrogantly.

"I'm ready," Daphne said to Sabrina. "But are you sure about this? The police are after us. Do you think going to the jailhouse is the smartest thing?"

"I don't see any other way," Sabrina said as she opened the front door. Hamstead scrambled off the car hood.

"Finally, you two have come to your senses," the sheriff said. He and his deputies hurried toward them.

Sabrina looked down at the carpet full of food hovering next to them. "Carpet, go to the police officers," she said. The carpet rose into the air and floated gently toward Hamstead and his men, and as it got closer it began to have the effect Sabrina hoped.

"Food!" one of the deputies squealed as the carpet stopped at their feet.

The smell of the cakes and pies sent a change through the two deputies, and soon both were in pig form, rooting wildly through the banquet.

"Gentlemen, we have work to do here!" Hamstead shouted while eyeing a pan of baked beans the others had overlooked. Unable to resist, he quickly shape-shifted to his pig form and slopped around in the mess.

Puck hovered several feet in the air near the girls, clearly displeased with Sabrina's success.

Daphne looked up at him and smiled. "We couldn't do this without you," she said, earning a grumpy shrug. "As soon as Jack tells us how to stop that giant, we're going to need you to lead us again."

The boy puffed up with pride, and a huge smile sprang to his face. He winked at Daphne, and then zipped across the front yard until he was hovering directly over the squad cars. The gorging piggies didn't even notice him.

Sabrina, Daphne, and Elvis stepped out of the house, closing the door behind them. With nimble fingers, Sabrina went to work locking all the bolts on the door, while Daphne kept an eye on Hamstead and his men.

"They're disgusting," Daphne said, mimicking the pigs' grunting and oinking.

"OK, that's the last one," Sabrina said, inserting the final key. She turned it and heard the lock roll into place.

"Ready?" she asked, pulling up the zipper on her sister's jacket.

"Ready!"

Sabrina turned to the pigs. "Carpet, here!"

Abruptly, the carpet pulled itself out from under the three pigs, sending them topsy-turvy and flopping across the yard. The food flew into the air and rained down on them with a great *splat* as the carpet itself glided across the yard and stopped at Sabrina's feet.

"Get them!" Hamstead shouted as he struggled onto his hoofs and then back into his human form. The deputies followed suit, and in no time they were all running toward the girls.

"Excuse me, piggies," Puck called from above. He blew a low note on his flute, and within seconds a wave of pixies flew out of the woods. He played another note, and the little lights encircled the two parked squad cars, effortlessly lifting each. They carried them high over the house and into several large trees, where they squeezed them between the thick branches. The police officers snorted their protests, but the boy just laughed.

The plan was working, and it was time for the girls to go. They stepped onto the carpet. "Hold on tight. We haven't actually ridden on this thing," Sabrina said. She and Daphne knelt down and each grabbed a side of the carpet. Elvis hopped on, too, and Daphne wrapped her free arm around his neck.

"Don't worry, Elvis. I've got you," the little girl said.

The police were almost on top of them when Sabrina shouted, "UP!" and the carpet rocketed into the sky. The girls held on for dear life as the house, the yard, and the street became smaller and smaller. Sabrina's stomach lurched as they found themselves shooting through a cloud.

"Carpet, down!" she said as the oxygen began to seep from her lungs. Just as quickly as the carpet rose, it fell. Daphne's pigtails lifted from the side of her head and floated next to her ears as the girls screeched back toward Earth, falling like a rock.

"CARPET, STOP!" Sabrina cried, inches before the carpet smashed onto the ground. She gasped with relief. Unfortunately, they stopped right behind the three police officers.

"Wait, we've forgotten something!" Daphne cried. "Carpet, take us to the front door."

"No!" Sabrina shouted, but it was too late. The magic carpet zipped off again, this time plowing into the group of portly police and knocking them down like bowling pins.

"What are you doing?" she demanded as the carpet screeched to a halt at the door of Granny's house.

"There's one more lock," Daphne said. She knocked on the door three times. "We'll be back!"

But the delay had given Hamstead and his men the time they needed to recover, and they now had the carpet surrounded.

Hamstead grabbed one of the tassels and smiled. "OK, fun time is over, girls," he said.

"Let go of the carpet," Sabrina demanded. Elvis echoed her protest with a low growl.

"Not a chance! Now, let's head down to the station and—"

"I said, let go of the carpet."

"What are you going to do to make me?" Hamstead scoffed.

Sabrina and Daphne exchanged glances. Daphne tightened her grip on the carpet and gave Elvis an extra squeeze.

"Carpet, up!" The carpet shot into the sky, carrying the girls, Elvis, and a stubborn Hamstead with it. Hanging on with one hand, the sheriff desperately tried to climb aboard as they soared high above the house.

"Take us down, right now!" he squealed. Sabrina peeked over the side and smirked.

"I'm sorry, Sheriff, but you don't have a ticket for this flight. I'm afraid you're going to have to get off at the next stop. Carpet, we have an unwanted passenger. Get rid of him!"

The carpet bolted forward as if thrilled with the request. It zipped up and down and did wide loop-the-loops that made Sabrina want to barf. She looked over at Daphne and Elvis, who both sat calmly on the carpet.

"If you just let go, it's a real easy ride," Daphne shouted over the whipping wind, but Sabrina wasn't convinced and she continued to hold on tight. A small beetle flew into her mouth, and she spat it out, gagging.

Unfortunately, Hamstead was still very much a passenger.

"Let go!" Sabrina shouted again, but the sheriff shook his head defiantly. Displaying its own stubbornness, the carpet darted over the house and began to skim the top of the forest. Hamstead smacked into limbs and skittered across treetops.

"I'm not going anywhere!" he shouted as the carpet found an opening in the forest and dove into it like a kamikaze pilot. Sabrina was sure it was going to sacrifice them all to get rid of its unwanted rider, but just as it seemed they would all be splattered across the forest floor, the carpet leveled out and dragged Hamstead directly over some thorny bushes. Motivated by the pain, the sheriff struggled once more to climb aboard.

"Carpet, do something!" Sabrina cried.

The carpet dove into the forest and zipped along a rocky stream. It lowered itself to mere inches above the water, dragging Hamstead along the muddy banks, and finally shaking him loose. He tumbled into the mud and sank up to his nose.

The carpet stopped and hovered above him as the sheriff crawled out of the muck. A small frog leaped from his shirt pocket as he wiped filth from his eyes.

As the girls darted away on the carpet, Sabrina could hear Boarman and Swineheart rushing to their boss's aid.

"Boss, what are you fooling around in the mud for?" Boarman asked.

"Shut up!"

The girls soared out of the forest and high into the sky. There, Puck met them and flew alongside, laughing at the sheriff's misfortune.

"You keep them busy!" Sabrina shouted, and the boy's face darkened.

Daphne pinched her sister. "You have to talk to him like he's the leader. He needs to feel he's important."

Sabrina was stunned by her sister's perceptiveness.

"Sorry, Puck. I know you can handle them, and we'll be back soon with all the information you will need," Daphne continued. "We know you could kill the giant yourself right now, but a little insider information never hurts."

Puck puffed up with pride. "Of course, it's probably a waste of time, but who knows? By the way, there's one more cop you have to deal with when you get there."

"Who?" Daphne asked.

"A nervous little man named Ichabod Crane."

"The guy from the Sleepy Hollow story?" Sabrina asked.

"That's him. Since he nearly lost his head, he gave up teaching and became a cop. I guess he thinks he's safer if he's around the police. He shouldn't be too much of a problem," Puck said, turning in midair and soaring away.

"How did you know we can get him to do whatever we want if we pretend he's in charge?" Sabrina asked Daphne.

"It's what I do with you," the little girl replied.

"Carpet, take us to Jack," Sabrina said after she stuck her tongue out at her sister.

The carpet glided above the little town. For the first time, Sabrina could see Ferryport Landing for what it really was—quaint. To the east of the town, the setting sun shone on the curve of the Hudson River, and old gas lamps flickered on along the path by the water. More lights twinkled in the center of the town, where dozens of brownstone buildings clustered around Main Street. Sabrina could see people having supper in the railway-car diner and watching a first movie at the drive-in theater. Far off to the west of town, she could just make out the humped shapes of the tree-blanketed mountains.

As they got closer to Main Street, the carpet began to descend, dropping nearly a dozen feet at once and causing Sabrina's belly to flip. She looked at her sister and saw that she had wrapped her arms around Elvis and was squeezing the air out of the poor dog.

When the carpet leveled out, Sabrina looked around and saw that they were floating next to the window of a brick building. It had bars on it. Suddenly a boyish face with spiky blond hair appeared. It was Jack! He had beautiful blue eyes and a button nose, but he looked tired and in desperate need of a shave. He also had a painful-looking fat lip.

"What's going on out there? Can't a man get some rest when he's in prison?" he shouted in a thick English accent. When he saw the girls, he lifted himself higher in order to see what they were standing on. Then he smiled.

"Well, young ladies . . . who might you be?"

"Are you Jack?" Sabrina asked.

"That's the name I was given," he replied with a chuckle.

"*The* Jack?" Daphne asked. "As in 'Jack and the Beanstalk'?"

"Indeed I am, duck. But as you can see, I'm a little indisposed to be signing autographs."

"We need your help!" Daphne cried.

"Well, I don't know if you happened to have noticed, but this isn't a country club I'm relaxing in. This is the town jail. Unless you need some help making license plates, I think you've got the wrong bloke."

"We need your help with a giant," Sabrina said.

Jack's eyes grew wide, and a smile briefly lit up his features. Then he grew terribly serious and pulled his face closer to the bars.

"A giant, you said?"

"He's taken our grandmother," Sabrina replied.

"And we want her back!" Daphne added.

"Well, I don't blame you," the young man said. "But exactly

how does a human go about getting herself in trouble with a giant?"

"We're Sabrina and Daphne Grimm. Our grandmother is—"

"Relda Grimm," Jack interrupted with a smirk. "I should have guessed. Went and got herself in trouble with a big boy, eh?"

"Yes, she and Mr. Canis both," Daphne said.

"Canis, eh? Can't say I feel sorry about that," Jack growled. "So what do you want from me?"

"We were told you're an expert on giants," Sabrina answered. "We need you to tell us everything you can about how to stop this one and save our family."

"It's true, I am an expert on the big boys. Killed nearly fifty of them in my day," Jack boasted.

"The books said it was less than twenty," Daphne said.

"Don't believe everything you read, duck," replied Jack. "I've sent more than my fair share of big boys to the grave. Why, there was a time when people used to call me Jack the Giant Killer. I was famous, oh yes. My name was once synonymous with bravery and daring, until the spell that trapped me in this barmy town."

"What does *barmy* mean?" Daphne whispered to her sister.

Sabrina shrugged. She was having trouble understanding Jack's accent.

"Now I'm taking any work I can. Do you know what the mighty Jack does for a living?"

Sabrina began to get nervous as the young man's face filled with rage. She knew the answer to his question but thought it best to lie. "No, I don't."

"I sell shoes and suits at Paul Bunyon's House of Big and Tall," Jack exploded. "A lowly salesboy! I sat with kings. I drank the finest wines in the world. I filled my belly with exotic meats and socialized with the world's most interesting people, and now I spend my days measuring inseams and helping people pick out insoles!"

"We're sorry," Daphne said.

"At least that's what I used to do. Today I quit!" Jack bragged. "I have a feeling Jack the Giant Killer's luck is going to change."

"So how did you end up in jail?" Sabrina asked.

"That miserable cur, Charming," Jack raged. "Runs this town like it's his own personal kingdom, and he wants to keep the rest of us as peasants."

"Did he give you the fat lip?" asked Sabrina.

"You bet!" Jack said, wiping his wound with a bloody handkerchief. "No worries. You can't keep a bloke like me down, can you? No siree, Bob! You can count on that!"

"Jack, I hate to interrupt, but we've really got to hurry. Is there anything you can tell us that will help?" Sabrina asked.

"Oh, I'm going to be a big help to you ladies," he said with a confident grin. "Just as soon as the two of you break me out of jail."

8

SABRINA GASPED.

"You want us to help you break out of prison?"

Jack nodded his head. "Quite right."

"How are we supposed to do that?" Sabrina asked.

"Easy. You go in through the front door and distract the guard. Then the little one here will hit him in the gob with a club or something and snatch his keys."

"I'm seven years old. I can't hit someone with a club, and not in the gob—whatever that is!" Daphne cried.

"Sure you can. Deputy Crane isn't going to put up a fight. He's daft in the head and jumpy as a flea. But if he does, all you have to do is hit him in the shins. He'll fall over like a sack of potatoes," Jack replied.

"She's not hitting anyone with a club," Sabrina said.

"Well, if saving your granny and her pal isn't that important to you, I can just stay in the nick."

Sabrina looked into Jack's hopeful face. How could this odd little man actually be the key to Granny and Mr. Canis's survival? It just didn't seem possible, but on the other hand, the note Granny had left told them that the mirror would have all the answers they needed. After two days of disbelieving everything the old woman had told her, Sabrina didn't feel like being proved wrong again, especially when so much was riding on the outcome.

"So, girls, what's it going to be? If I could do it myself, I would've already, but the bobby took my lock-picking kit when he put the cuffs on me. Smart on his part, too. There isn't a door Jack can't open."

"We'll get you out of here, but we're going to do it my way," Sabrina declared. "No one is going to get hurt. Deal?"

Jack frowned but thrust his hand out the window. He shook Sabrina's and smiled. "So, boss, what's the plan?"

"First, I'm going to need your shirt."

When Sabrina opened the front door to the police station, her heart was pounding faster than ever. They were taking a huge chance, especially with Sheriff Hamstead and his deputies searching for them. By now Crane had to know the girls were on the loose. Two kids dressed in bright orange monkey sweatshirts, flying around on a magic carpet with a two-hundred-pound Great Dane, weren't going to be too hard to spot. On the upside, what they were about to do was the sneakiest thing the girls had ever tried. It was nice to be challenged every once in awhile.

When the door swung open, Sabrina half expected to find Hamstead, Boarman, and Swineheart waiting for them. But luckily, the station was empty except for a tall, painfully thin man with a gigantic hooked nose, thin lips, and an Adam's apple that bobbed up and down. Ichabod Crane looked just like the story described him, and he was fast asleep, sitting in a chair with his feet propped up on his desk.

Sabrina found the light switch and flipped it off, drowning the room in murkiness. She gestured behind her, and the carpet drifted in, hovering two feet off the ground and carrying its own Headless Horseman: Daphne, sitting on Elvis's back and wearing Jack's shirt so that her head was hidden inside.

"He's going to figure this out," Daphne whispered.

"It's our only shot," Sabrina replied. She crouched down behind an empty desk and cupped her hands around her mouth. She kicked the door shut, and it slammed so loudly the poor man fell backward over his chair. Once he was on his hands and knees, he rubbed his eyes and looked around in the dark.

"Who's there?" he called in a whiny, high-pitched voice.

"Crane!" Sabrina moaned in the deepest voice she could produce. The carpet slowly drifted across the room, carrying its headless passenger.

"You!" the deputy cried in horror. "You're supposed to be gone!"

"I have returned," Sabrina croaked. The dark room was creating a very believable nightmare. Crane scurried around the room, hiding behind desks and chairs the best he could.

"Crane, you cannot hide from me. I am the Headless Horseman. I see all!"

"I'm a law enforcement officer now!" Crane shouted, trying to muster all his courage. "A defender of the peace. I can arrest you for . . . for . . . riding a horse without a head. That's a serious crime in this town."

"Your laws mean nothing to me. I've come for something, Crane, and I will have it!" Sabrina bellowed.

"What do you want?" the deputy cried.

"Your head!" Sabrina groaned.

Crane burst into tears. "No! Please, not my head!" he begged.

"Very well. If not your head, I'll take something else."

"Anything, anything. Whatever you want!"

"I want the keys to the jail."

Crane was silent for several moments.

"Why do you want the keys?"

"Would you prefer I take your head instead?" Sabrina moaned, just as an unlucky bounce of the carpet knocked Daphne off Elvis's back. She fell to the ground, toppling a trash can into a radiator. The sound couldn't have been more appropriate, but Daphne was down for the count. Unable to see, she flailed in her costume, causing more commotion and sending a computer crashing to the floor.

Crane, who seemed to think this was part of the Headless Horseman's attack, shouted, "Here, the keys!" and tossed them at Daphne's feet.

"Now go, before I change my mind!" Sabrina said. Crane leaped to his feet and ran, not noticing her as he rushed out the station door. Once she was sure he was gone, Sabrina stood up and turned on the lights. Daphne was still rolling around, unable to see anything.

"Get me out of this," the little girl begged. Sabrina unhooked the top buttons of Jack's shirt, and Daphne's head popped up. Elvis immediately licked her face.

"You were very convincing." Sabrina laughed as she helped her sister to her feet.

Daphne growled. "Let's break Jack out of here."

Sabrina rolled up the carpet and flung it over her shoulder, and the two girls raced to find Jack. Down a long hallway at the back of the building were two jail cells. The one on the left was empty, but the one on the right held Jack. He stood with his arms reaching through the bars as the girls approached.

"Corking! I told you it would work!" he cheered. "Now get me out of here."

Sabrina handed Jack the keys, and he sorted through them. He found the right one, stuck it in the lock, and turned it from inside. The door clicked, and he pushed it open.

Elvis lunged angrily at the cell. Growling and barking wildly, the big dog sniffed and snarled at Jack.

"Elvis, it's OK, he's a friend," Daphne said, which seemed to calm the dog down, but he continued sniffing, at full alert.

"Crane ran like he'd seen the devil himself," Sabrina said proudly.

"I've seen the devil, and you're not him," a voice said from down the hallway.

Sabrina turned and found Deputy Crane standing in the doorway, blocking their exit. He was so angry he was shaking.

"Get back in your cell, Jack," the deputy ordered, pulling his billy club from its strap and swinging it threateningly.

"Sorry, Ichy. I wish I could help you, but I've got other plans. Now, are you going to let us pass, or are we going to have to get rough?" Jack threatened.

Daphne grabbed his undershirt and yanked on it. "You promised—no one gets hurt."

Jack scowled. "I wouldn't hurt him . . . much," he said.

"Bring it on, you washed-up has-been."

Jack laughed. "That's what I am? A washed-up has-been? I'd watch what you say, Ichy. Things can change in the blink of an eye."

"Not in Ferryport Landing, Jack."

"Carpet, let's wrap this up!" Jack commanded, and the carpet lifted off Sabrina's shoulder. It darted down the hallway and, like an anaconda, wrapped Crane inside it. He fumbled and fought but couldn't break free.

Jack walked over to the rug and patted it lightly.

"Nothing personal, Ichy, but destiny awaits," he said. He grabbed an end of the carpet and pulled it roughly, causing Crane to spin away like a top. After several rotations, the skinny man collapsed to the floor, overcome by dizziness.

Jack set the carpet on the floor and stepped onto it.

"All right, ladies," he said as he extended his hand to help the girls onto the rug. Elvis rushed to join them and stood like a guard between the girls and Jack.

"Carpet, up," Sabrina said, and it rose a few feet and then sank slowly back down like a balloon with a hole in it.

"Why aren't we going up?" Daphne cried.

"We must be too heavy!" Jack groaned. "Can we lose the hound?"

Elvis answered him with a threatening snarl.

"Very well. Carpet, take us to the Grimm house!"

Though it was weighed down, the carpet didn't lack any of its speed. It zipped along, three feet off the floor, down the hallway, through the main room, and out the front door of the police station. It sailed across the parking lot and made a left into the street, causing a pickup truck to screech to a stop. As they passed, the girls waved a friendly "Sorry" gesture to the bewildered driver.

"That was almost too easy," Jack said. But no sooner had he puffed out his chest than the sound of a siren wailed in their ears. A moment later, a police car turned the corner and raced in the group's direction. Ichabod Crane was behind the wheel.

"Tenacious, isn't he?" Jack said.

"*Tenacious*?" Daphne asked.

"It means persistent," Sabrina said.

"And what does *persistent* mean?" Daphne asked.

"It means he's not going to give up."

"And I wouldn't have it any other way," Jack assured them. "Carpet, faster!"

"Is this the best idea?" Sabrina shouted, holding on to an end of the carpet as they raced between cars and ran through a red light. "We're attracting a lot of attention!"

"It's about time this little burg saw some action!" Jack cried out happily. "Ferryport Landing, you haven't seen anything yet!"

Sabrina heard a horrible crunching sound behind them and turned back to see what could have made such a loud noise. What she saw stole the breath from her lungs. The road behind them began to rise, like a massive wave rolling in from the ocean. It was followed by another horrible crunching sound. She watched parked cars get tossed aside like toys.

"We're in luck, ladies," Jack said. "We've already found our giant."

Suddenly an enormous foot planted itself in the middle of Main Street. The impact caused windows in nearby businesses to shatter. The ground exploded, and a gas main underneath the street burst, shooting flames high into the air.

"What do we do?" Daphne cried.

"We have two choices. Stand and fight and die a horrible, messy death, or run," Jack replied.

"Carpet, get us out of here!" Sabrina shouted, and the little rug sped away.

Unfortunately, the giant was not discouraged by how fast the group was making its getaway. A single stride put the monster right behind them, even when the rug increased its speed again. And with every step the big monster took, the pavement crumbled beneath him. Electrical wires snapped, spraying sparks everywhere. The few drivers on the road at that late hour lost control of their cars and crashed into buildings. Jack turned to see the chaos and grinned broadly.

"Finally, this is getting interesting." He laughed.

The carpet took a sharp left turn and Sabrina felt lucky that she hadn't tumbled off, when she noticed that Daphne was no longer sitting next to her. In fact, Daphne was hanging from the back of the carpet, holding on desperately with both hands.

"Jack!" Sabrina cried. The spiky-haired fellow reached down and grabbed the little girl by the back of her sweatshirt and hauled her onto the carpet.

"Blimey! This is better than a roller coaster." Jack laughed again as he set the girl safely on the carpet.

Daphne hugged her sister. It was the first time Sabrina had ever felt her sister shake from fear. She didn't like it.

"We're going to get ourselves killed," she shouted as the carpet narrowly missed being crushed by a delivery truck filled with chickens.

"Nonsense, we can't die like this. We're immortal," Jack replied.

"*You're* immortal—we're not. We have to get off this road," Sabrina demanded.

"I see. Must be quite a pain to be human, but the carpet picks the route." Just then an eighteen-wheeler pulled directly into their path and stopped.

"CARPET, UP!" everyone shouted. The carpet slowly rose, sputtering as if it were the little train that couldn't.

"We're not going to make it!" Sabrina shouted.

"Lie down flat," Jack commanded.

"You can't mean what I think you mean!"

Jack nodded, and the two girls reluctantly lay on their backs.

"Elvis, play dead," Daphne said, and the dog lay on his side. The little girl turned a worried face to her sister. "He's not going to do what I think he is, is he?"

"CARPET, DOWN!" Jack shouted, and the carpet fell from the sky until it was literally skidding across the pavement. Its momentum carried the group underneath the truck to the other side and down the street. When they sat up again, the young man was already laughing—until he looked up and saw the street cleaner barreling toward them.

"CARPET, UP!" they all shouted, and the little rug struggled higher, narrowly missing the boiling-hot water and sharp bristles the machine used to scour the street. The carpet continued to rise until it cleared the vehicle. Sabrina turned and saw Ichabod Crane was out of his car, angrily ordering the drivers of the eighteen-wheeler and the street cleaner to move. Unfortunately, the traffic problems did little to stop the giant. Its monstrous foot soared high above the commotion and landed only yards from the carpet.

"THAT THING IS GOING TO KILL SOMEONE!" Sabrina shouted. "Carpet, we have to get away from the main road!"

The carpet made an abrupt turn toward Ferryport Landing's farm community. The giant followed closely behind, and the little rug dodged each deadly footfall. Several times the ugly brute reached out to squash the group in his hands, but each time the carpet zipped out of his reach. He grunted and beat on his chest but eventually gave up, shaking his fist in the air with frustration.

"Don't cry, big boy," Jack shouted to the giant as he disappeared behind them on the horizon. "You'll be seeing me again very soon!"

As the magic carpet coasted up the driveway, it was barely six inches off the ground and seemed to have lost all of its kick. When the group finally stepped off of it, the beautiful little rug dropped to the ground and rolled itself up, just as it had been delivered to the girls. Daphne leaned over and picked it up gingerly, the way one would a tired kitten, and cradled it in her arms.

"Poor thing is all worn out," she said, cooing.

Sabrina looked toward the forest. Hamstead's squad cars were still perched in the tall trees behind the house, but he and his men were nowhere to be seen. Reaching into her pocket, Sabrina removed Granny Relda's enormous key ring and began the tedious job of unlocking all the bolts. Jack watched attentively until she had unlocked every one. Before Sabrina could say the magic words that gained them entrance, Daphne pulled her aside, cupped her hand over her big sister's ear, and whispered, "Should we let him in?"

It was a fair question. When they didn't listen to Granny Relda, they regretted it, but they were in a tough situation. Letting Puck inside had turned out fine. Why not Jack? Plus, he was probably the only person in the world who could confront a giant.

"I don't think we have much of a choice," Sabrina whispered back. She made a fist and knocked on the door. "We're home."

Jack cocked an eyebrow in confusion.

"Family tradition," Sabrina said in hopes of throwing him off. "Granny does it and it makes Daphne laugh, so I picked it up, too."

Daphne faked a laugh.

Jack shrugged. "Whatever."

"What's he doing here?" Puck said as he floated down from the sky.

Jack turned around and eyed the flying boy, whose huge wings flapped hard to allow him to hover over them.

"He's offered to help," Daphne explained, but this time her diplomacy fell on deaf ears.

"Help us do what—try on some big pants?" Puck sneered. "You weren't supposed to bring him back."

"Listen, you little brat, I'm the only hope you've got," Jack replied. "Two little girls and a garden gnome aren't going to stop a giant."

"Who are you calling a garden gnome, you insolent peasant?" Puck said, pulling his flute from his sweatshirt.

"Boys!" Sabrina and Daphne cried in unison. "That's enough!"

Puck and Jack backed off. The girls looked at each other. Apparently, there was a bit of Granny in them both.

"What happened to Hamstead and his deputies?" Sabrina asked.

"Charming came by and picked them up," Puck said, staring a hole into Jack. "I sat up on the roof and watched him scream at them for half an hour. It was hilarious."

"Good. We don't need them getting in the way," Sabrina said, turning and opening the front door.

Elvis rushed past her and into the kitchen, returning a moment later with Granny Relda's handbag. He dropped it at the girls' feet and began to snarl at it. The girls ignored him. Daphne headed into the living room, set the carpet tenderly on the floor, and plopped down, exhausted, into a chair. She pulled a book out from underneath the cushion she was sitting on and tossed it aside.

"So this is the legendary Grimm house," Jack said as he wandered from room to room, peeking behind photographs and snooping around. "Oh, I wish I had my camera with me. No one will believe I was actually here."

"Make yourself at home, please," Sabrina said. If Jack heard the sarcasm in her voice, he pretended not to and continued his snooping.

"So, girls, where can I take a kip?" he asked.

Daphne looked at Sabrina for a definition, but Sabrina shook her head.

"I have no idea what that means."

"You know, hit the sack?" Jack said.

"You want to go take a nap?"

"I'm zonked."

"We didn't break you out of jail so you could camp out in our house."

"Kids, I was on a lumpy jail cot all night. I need to get some rest if I'm going to take care of your very big problem, and besides, my plan can't go into effect until tomorrow night."

"Tomorrow night! Granny and Mr. Canis could be dead by then," Daphne said.

"Only if the big boy gets hungry," Jack said casually. "I wouldn't worry too much. There're lots of things to eat in the forests."

Sabrina watched Puck shake his head in disgust. He clearly thought Jack was a con artist, and she was starting to feel the same way.

"What's your plan?" she asked.

"Right now, it's best that we don't discuss it." Jack fell onto the couch and stretched his arms behind his head. "We'll talk about it later. I just need a couple of hours of shut-eye."

"He doesn't have a plan!" Puck snapped.

Puck looked at the girls, turned, and stomped toward the door.

The girls chased after him. "Where are you going?" Daphne asked.

"What do you care?" he complained bitterly. "You've got your giant killer. Good luck!"

He slammed the door behind him.

"What do we do now?" Daphne asked sleepily.

Sabrina eyed Jack from the hall. He was already snoring.

"I suppose we might as well get some rest, too," Sabrina said, seeing her sister's head droop. She scooped her grandmother's handbag off the floor and set it on the table, then gently urged Daphne out of her chair. Elvis whined at the girls.

Sabrina turned and whispered into the dog's ear, "Elvis, keep an eye on Jack."

The dog's eyes reflected an understanding, and he seated himself like a stone guardian, watching the sleeping man. The two girls went up to their bedroom. It had been a long day.

Sabrina didn't remember falling asleep, but when she woke up she was still in her clothes and it was already nine o'clock in the morning. She crawled out of bed, leaving her snoring sister alone, and walked down the hallway. She heard a sound from Granny Relda's room and decided to investigate, but when she opened the door, no one was there.

She stepped inside and noticed a framed photo on the old

woman's dresser. It was of Relda and Basil, hugging happily under an apple tree. As usual, Mr. Canis was standing nearby. His face seemed slightly out of focus, and the camera flash had turned his eyes a bright blue color. Sabrina reached into her pocket and pulled out the photo she'd found in Granny Relda's handbag. Comparing the two, she found the same odd effect in Mr. Canis's eyes. Sabrina was surprised she hadn't noticed it before.

"What are you doing in here?" Puck's voice startled Sabrina, and she dropped both the framed and unframed photos to the ground. Luckily, the glass didn't break. Sabrina looked around the room, searching for the boy, but she didn't see him.

"Up here, ugly," said Puck.

Sabrina looked up and nearly screamed. A housefly the size of Elvis was sitting upside down on the ceiling above her. But its enormous size wasn't nearly as disturbing as its human head, which had shaggy blond hair, a gold crown, and a mischievous grin. Apparently, Puck had a whole bag of upsetting tricks.

"*What are you doing in here*?" Sabrina demanded.

"Uh . . . it's the only quiet room in the house," Puck replied. "Besides, I know you and Jack have your big plans. Wouldn't want to get in the way."

"Could you come down here?"

Puck suddenly morphed back into his human form and fell clumsily to the bed below.

"You're being a baby," Sabrina said. "Jack wants to help, and you can't stand not being the center of attention."

"Whatever," the boy replied. "But when he gets you into trouble, don't be angry when I remind you that I told you so."

"If you have a better plan, then let's hear it, 'cause all I've heard from you is the never-ending buzz of your flapping lips," Sabrina snapped. "My parents ran out on me and Daphne almost two years ago. We've been through the wringer and have been bounced around for far too long. I admit, when we met Granny Relda, I didn't want anything to do with her. But now that I know she's the real deal, I'm going to do whatever it takes to get her back. I've lost one family. I'm not losing another!"

"Don't look at me," Puck said. "I made no promises to the old lady. She knew I was trouble when we met."

Sabrina was taken aback by his insensitivity. "So you couldn't care less what happens to her?"

"I've learned one thing in this life. Look out for yourself. Everyone else will just end up disappointing you."

"So you won't help?"

"You've already got one giant killer," Puck said.

Suddenly the sound of Elvis's barking filled the room. Sabrina peered into the hallway. There she saw Jack fighting with Elvis, who was shredding the man's pants in his angry teeth.

"Get this beast away from me!" Jack begged. "He's rabid!"

"What are you doing up here?" Sabrina asked suspiciously.

"I was coming to wake you."

Daphne entered the hallway rubbing sleep from her eyes. "What's going on?"

"The giant killer is prowling around the house looking for something to steal," Puck said. "Your savior has sticky fingers."

"Shut your mouth, you dirty little hooligan!" Jack shouted.

"Your compliments will get you nowhere."

"Elvis, calm down," Daphne said as she patted the angry dog on the head—her touch seemed to have a soothing effect on him. "Take a chill pill."

Elvis released Jack's pant leg.

"Thank you," Jack said, eyeing his mangled trousers. "So, are you ready to hear my plan?"

Sabrina looked at Puck, hoping the boy might reconsider and help them, but he sneered and looked away.

"Yes, we're ready," she replied.

Puck said nothing. He walked down the stairs. Sabrina heard the door close behind him.

"Little bugger was getting in the way," Jack said. "Is anyone hungry? Let's have some breakfast!" He rushed down the stairs and into the kitchen, the girls following behind. They watched as he riffled through the contents of the refrigerator.

"There's nothing real to eat in this house," Jack complained. "I could really go for some bubble-and-squeak or some bangers. Do you ducks think you could cook up some steak-and-kidney pie for me?"

The girls stared.

"I hear noises coming from his mouth, but they don't sound like words," Daphne said.

"Maybe he's having some kind of fit," Sabrina said.

Jack rolled his eyes, snatched up some leftovers, and ate greedily.

"Let me tell you lasses," he said, his mouth full, "jail food is terrible."

"We'll take your word for it," Sabrina said.

While Jack ate, the girls took turns telling him how Granny Relda and Mr. Canis had been kidnapped. Sabrina told him her theory about Mayor Charming being the mysterious Mr. Englishman, and how she thought he was using the giant to scare people off their land.

"So, tell us your plan," Daphne said as Jack finished his breakfast.

"I'm still working out the details."

Both the girls flashed Jack an angry look.

"Don't worry!" he said defensively. "It's going to be brilliant."

Sabrina sighed and got up from her seat to grab the telephone.

"We helped you escape from jail so you could help us save

our grandmother, and all you've done is eat our food and drool on our sofa. If you can't do it, then I'm just going to call Deputy Crane and let him know you're ready to go back!" she threatened.

"Put the phone down and relax," Jack said calmly as he helped himself to another chicken leg. "You think tracking down a giant is easy? Giants have survived thousands of years being as big as they are, and they've learned a few things about staying out of sight. Now, we can traipse through the woods, cut down the forest, and drag the Hudson River, but the fact is that if a giant doesn't want to be found, he's not going to be found."

"You're talking in circles," Sabrina complained.

"What I'm saying, duck, is we need to use our heads. Think about what we know so far. The mayor is trying to buy up the entire town, and what better way than to get a giant to scare off the landowners who won't sell to him? So when your family started snooping around, he sent the big boy after you. He's got your granny, and now he's after the two of you."

"Go on," Sabrina said as she set the phone back in its cradle.

"Applebee's can't be the only farm Charming wants to buy. I bet he's got a map of Ferryport Landing in his office with all the properties he's after. If we get a look at it, I bet we could see where the giant will strike next. I bet the map will even tell us where the giant is hiding. All you have to do is sneak into his office during the ball tonight, find the map, and bingo-bango, we kill the big boy and save your grandmum."

"*That's* your plan?" Sabrina cried.

"You got something better? I know that sneaking into the ball doesn't sound as exciting as burning down the forest and waiting for the giant to run out, but I've always believed the easiest way is the best way."

"There's one big problem, though," Daphne spoke up. "The mayor and the police are looking for you. You're going to have a tough time sneaking into the mansion."

"Oh, girls, I'm not going. You are."

"Us?"

"We can't go into that party. They're looking for us, too!" Sabrina cried.

"Don't worry. You'll be fine. In fact, you're going to go right through the front door and no one is even going to notice," Jack said confidently. "I don't suppose you've got a map of the mansion around here, do you?"

As their "hero" rested, the girls frantically searched the books for a blueprint of Charming's estate. Eventually, in one of their grandfather Basil's many journals, they found a sketch of a rough plan of the house.

The mayor's mansion was a sprawling several-story palace with dozens of rooms. Their grandpa had given estimates of room sizes, locations of various windows, and even an indication of where he believed there was a secret passage. But he hadn't seen the entire house, and many parts of the drawing were labeled with question marks. Sabrina noticed he paid extra attention to possible escape routes—apparently, their grandpa had been a bit of a sneak, too.

Sabrina carefully studied the map and did her best to commit it to memory. When Jack finally woke up, several hours later, he found the girls ready to get started.

"Let's go see your mirror," Jack said.

"I don't know what you're talking about," Sabrina said, stealing a look into Daphne's eyes.

"Girls, everyone knows Relda has the magic mirror. Why do you think the front door has a dozen locks on it?"

Sabrina took the keys out of her pocket and led her sister and their guest up the steps. Once they arrived at the mirror's room, she inserted the key and unlocked the door. As before, the face in the mirror appeared with a thunderstorm behind it.

"WHO DARES?" he bellowed.

"Turn off the drama, Mirror," Jack scoffed.

"Oh, it's you," Mirror mumbled.

"Of course it's me. I'm the bloke you call when you have a big problem," Jack bragged. "And these girls have a really big problem."

"And where is the flying carpet?" Mirror asked Sabrina.

"Sorry," she said. She walked to the doorway and called for it. After a couple of minutes, the carpet floated limply into the room.

"What have you done to it?" Mirror cried as the carpet fell to the floor and once again rolled itself up.

"I think we had too many people on it," Daphne explained as Mirror's hand broke the surface of the reflection and snatched the carpet from the ground.

"It's nearly unraveling in my hand," he wailed as he babied the rug. "Poor little carpet, look at how they treated you. Girls, the things we store here are priceless and one of a kind. You really need to take good care of them."

"Save your lecture for later, Mirror," Jack said. "We need to sneak into Charming's mansion tonight, and we need some disguises."

"Perhaps you should go to a costume shop."

"And we need the slippers."

"A-a-absolutely n-n-not," Mirror stammered.

"Listen, this house is going to be surrounded with the police any minute now. We need the slippers," Jack argued.

"Mrs. Grimm would not approve. The slippers were entrusted to this family so they would never fall into the wrong hands," Mirror replied.

"You can trust me," said Jack.

"Didn't you used to have your own magic items? What happened to the Cloak of Darkness?"

"I lost it in a poker game."

"You lost a cloak that turns you invisible in a poker game? What about the Shoes of Swiftness?"

"I hocked them."

"The Cap of Knowledge? The Goose That Laid the Golden Egg?"

"Lost the cap in the wind. And I accidentally left the window open one day and the goose flew off."

"I suppose you sold the Sword of Sharpness?" Mirror grumbled.

"No, I still have the Sword of Sharpness," said Jack indignantly. "I just misplaced it. It's in my flat somewhere. The point is, we need the slippers. If you won't let me have them, then let one of the girls. It doesn't make any difference to me."

"What slippers?" Sabrina shouted. She was tired of their bickering.

"Dorothy's slippers!" Jack and Mirror shouted back.

"Dorothy from *The Wonderful Wizard of Oz*?" Daphne exclaimed.

"Yes," Jack said impatiently. "They can transport you anywhere you want to go, all you have to do is—"

"Click three times!" Daphne cried. "Gimme the slippers!"

"Girls, I have to warn you. The slippers are very powerful magic. There are still those . . . some in this town . . . who would slit your throats to possess them," Mirror said.

"We'll be careful," Jack said, and then he did something that shocked Sabrina. He stepped into the reflection and pushed the man in the mirror aside.

"How dare you!" Mirror shouted.

"C'mon, ducks, keep up!" Jack said as his face appeared in the reflection.

The girls were unsure of what to do. Daphne reached up and curled her hand into her sister's. Sabrina squeezed softly, and the two of them took a tentative step through the mirror. It was an odd sensation, almost as if they were caught in a summer rainstorm, and when they finally opened their eyes, a brilliant glimmering light flooded their pupils. What they saw made Sabrina queasy. It wasn't natural. It just wasn't possible, and her brain struggled to understand.

Sabrina had half expected to walk into a perfect reflection of the room they had just left. After all, the mirror was a mirror. But she couldn't have been more wrong. Instead, she found herself in a long, wide hallway that reminded her of Grand Central Terminal. It was vast, with a vaulted ceiling and endless archways of glass and steel. Glowing marble columns held up the ceiling, which rose hundreds of feet above them. Breathtaking sculptures of men and monsters lined the hall. And along each wall were hundreds of doors of all shapes and sizes, some no bigger than a rabbit, others a hundred feet high. Some were wooden, others steel, and still others seemed to be made from pure light. Sabrina looked down at Granny Relda's key ring and finally understood why there were so many. Yet another of Granny's eccentricities had a legitimate explanation.

Even more startling than the gigantic room they were standing in was the man who lived in it. The face in the mirror was no longer a disembodied head. Gone was the intimidating visage. The man who stood before her was short and chubby, and he wore a suit and tie.

"This is outrageous. Keep your hands in your pockets, Jack," Mirror insisted.

"Mirror, I am shocked. Don't you trust me?" Jack said.

"I trust you about as much as the person who gave you that fat lip," said Mirror.

"What is this place?" Daphne asked.

"It's an arcana-powered, multiphasic, transdimensional pocket universe," Mirror replied.

"A what-who?"

"Your grandmother calls it the world's biggest walk-in closet," the little man explained. "It's a sort of holding area for dangerous and valuable items. I call it the Hall of Wonders, and you're not supposed to be in here."

"Oh, Mirror," Jack said. "We've learned one of your secrets. Don't worry, I'm sure you have a million more."

The little man's face flushed with anger. His fists clenched and he looked as if he might hit Jack, but the giant killer just ignored him.

"All right, Mirror, where are the slippers?" Jack asked impatiently.

"I still have reservations about this plan," Mirror complained.

"If the girls tell you to give them to us, can you resist?" Jack asked.

Mirror sighed and frowned. "No."

Jack tilted his head toward Sabrina.

"Can we at least look?" Sabrina asked.

"This way," Mirror said, gesturing for them to follow. He walked down the long hall past many doors. The plaque on one read FAIRY GODMOTHER WANDS while the next read TALKING PLANTS. As they continued down the hallway, they passed more doors. They were labeled POISONOUS FRUITS, DRAGON EGGS, IMPOSSIBLE ANIMALS, WISHING WELLS, CRYSTAL BALLS, CURSED TREASURE, SCROLLS AND PROPHESIES, and on and on and on. Passing one massive door, the group jumped as violent pounding from within threatened to knock it off its hinges. Something on the other side wanted out, something named GRENDEL.

The group pressed on down the hallway until they finally stopped at a door that read MAGIC SHOES.

"Here we are," Mirror said reluctantly. "But I must once again remind you that magic is dangerous. There's a reason why the Everafters asked this family to look after all of these items. Magic in the wrong hands only leads to chaos."

"We'll be careful," said Sabrina as she knelt down to the lock. It was a simple one that would take a skeleton key, but Granny's key ring had dozens of skeleton keys. Sabrina tried the first one and it failed. She tried another; still nothing.

"Let me try," Jack said impatiently.

"I've got it," Sabrina snapped. She turned another key, and this time the lock opened. The door swung wide, and they all entered.

The room was simple, but its contents were amazing. Along the walls were hundreds of pairs of shoes: cowboy boots, woven sandals, wooden clogs, leather moccasins, and many more, all displayed on wooden shelves. Some of the shoes seemed as if they were made for animals, while others were big enough for the entire group to stand in. One golden pair had downy white wings that flapped as if the shoes were alive, and another glittering pair was made of pure glass.

Jack picked up the pair of shoes with wings, but Mirror promptly smacked his hand and snatched them from his grip. After replacing the shoes, Mirror crossed the room, picked up a pair of sparkling slippers, and handed them to Sabrina.

"Try to take better care of these than you did the magic carpet," he said gruffly.

If these were the famous ruby slippers, they were more silver than red, though in the light Sabrina saw hints of a warm, rosy color. She couldn't figure out what they were made of, but if forced to guess, she would have said tinfoil.

"Put them on, lass," Jack said.

"They're way too small," Sabrina said as she eyed the shoes.

"One size fits all, duck," Jack said.

Sabrina yanked off her sneakers and slid her foot inside one of the slippers, which magically grew in size and fit her perfectly. Once she eased her other foot into the second shoe she felt an odd energy shoot up her legs and fill her whole body.

Just then, Jack let out a howl and darted out of the room and across the hall.

"Jack!" Mirror shouted after him, but Jack didn't listen. When he and the girls finally found him, the giant killer was eyeing a door with a plaque that read MAGIC BEANS.

"I can't believe you have a whole room of them!" he shouted with glee.

"We might be bending the rules on the slippers, but those are off-limits to the likes of you!" Mirror said.

"How about a peek?" Jack pleaded. He suddenly looked like a lost little boy. "These things are part of my past. Can't a man take a walk down memory lane?"

Sabrina could see his expression, and all at once she felt

sorry for him. Jack was a man whom the whole world celebrated. He had seen amazing things and lived life to the fullest, but being trapped in Ferryport Landing had put an end to all of it. It dawned on Sabrina that Ferryport Landing might have been the home of many of the world's fairy-tale creatures, but it was also a prison they were never allowed to leave. It didn't seem right.

Sabrina pulled out the keys, knelt down, eyed the keyhole, and within seconds opened the door. Jack pushed past her into the tiny room, where a single mason jar sat on a table. Inside it was a collection of little white beans.

Jack gasped and picked up the jar. "There must be a hundred of them."

Mirror snatched the jar out of his hand and placed it back on the table.

"These things are dangerous. If you dropped them on the floor, we'd be ear-deep in giants."

Jack scowled for a moment and looked as if he were ready to fight for his treasure, but he took a deep breath and his anger vanished, replaced with a boyish grin.

"Thanks, Grimms. You don't know what you've done for me," he said.

Mirror hurried everyone back through the door.

"Well, ladies, now that we've got the shoes, we need the proper disguises," Jack said. "I think a little fairy godmother magic will do the trick."

"Wands are over here," Mirror said, leading them down the hallway. They stopped at the door labeled FAIRY GODMOTHER WANDS, and Sabrina unlocked it. Inside sat a small black cauldron with several wands sticking out of it. Mirror reached into the pot, removed one with a glittery glass star on the end, and handed it to Sabrina.

"The first magical item your family ever confiscated," Mirror said.

"I remember old Wilhelm Grimm trying to get that away from her." Jack laughed. "Girls, I'll say one thing about your family. They are brave. Fairy godmothers are sweet as pie, but try to take away their wands and they can get downright mean."

"Indeed," Mirror said.

"How does this work?" Sabrina asked.

Mirror frowned. "I can't believe your father!" he cried. "I'd hoped that your mother, Veronica, might at least have given you the basics behind his back. Very well, this is a makeover wand. It will alter your clothes, shoes, even your bodies, in any way you choose, with just a flick of the wrist."

"Why do we need a makeover?" Daphne asked, looking down at her orange monkey sweatshirt. "We look amazing!"

"You need to look like an Everafter. Charming's ball is going to be filled to the rafters with them, and you have to fit in," Jack said. "No humans."

Daphne smiled. "I know what I want to be! I want to be the Tin Woodsman!"

"Are you sure, honey?" the little man in the mirror asked. "Tin is so last season."

Daphne nodded enthusiastically.

"Very well, it's your fashion funeral," he said. "Sabrina, just say *Tin Woodsman,* make three small circles with the wand, and then tap her on the head."

"OK," Sabrina said. "Tin Woodsman!" She made three awkward circles in the air and then smacked her sister on the head with the wand. Daphne squealed in pain and rubbed the spot, but as she was rubbing, a miraculous change began to occur. Her skin took on a silvery tone. She grew several feet taller, and her clothes faded, only to be replaced by gears and joints. Her hair retreated into her scalp and a shiny funnel took its place. Sabrina blinked her eyes to be sure they weren't playing tricks on her, but she knew they weren't. Her sister had become the Tin Woodsman.

"That hurt," Daphne cried as her hand scraped against her new metallic head. Hearing the screech of metal in her ears, she looked at her hand and squealed in delight. She walked around the hall, squeaking with every step. "Look at me!"

"Spitting image," Jack said.

Daphne took the wand from her sister. "OK, who do you want to be?"

Sabrina was stumped. She realized she had to choose wisely. She needed to be inconspicuous at the ball, someone small and unnoticeable, and someone who could be very, very sneaky.

"OK, I was thinking . . ."

"I know—Momma Bear!" the little girl interrupted, and before Sabrina could stop her, she performed the circles and cracked her big sister on the head.

Sabrina felt the transformation immediately, as if her body were being inflated. Her clothes disappeared and were replaced with a bright, pink-and-white polka-dotted dress that ended well above her knee. She looked down at her humongous arms and groaned as hair exploded from every pore. Fangs burst from the top of her mouth, and razor-sharp claws sprang from her fingers and toes. She could feel them scratching at the insides of the ruby slippers, which expanded to fit her new size-26 feet. When the transformation was complete, Daphne giggled.

"You did that on purpose!" Sabrina growled.

"You're so cute!" Daphne cried as she threw her metal arms around her sister and gave her a big hug. "I could just eat you!"

"Well, no one's going to see the two of you coming," Jack moaned, though it was obvious he found the whole thing funny.

"Girls, you realize there's a timer with a makeover wand. When the clock strikes nine o'clock, you're going to change back. Do you understand?" Mirror lectured.

"Nine o'clock? Cinderella's fairy godmother gave her until midnight," Sabrina argued.

"Cinderella was seventeen years old. You are eleven. There's no way your grandmother would approve of your staying out until the wee hours of the morning."

"I don't think she'd mind, since we're trying to save her life!"

"That doesn't give us much time—it's seven o'clock right now," Jack said, eyeing his wristwatch.

Mirror took the wand from Daphne and put it back into the pot. He led the group out of the room, closed the door, and, when Sabrina couldn't manage, locked it with Granny's keys.

"One last thing," Jack said. "You don't happen to have any walkie-talkies in this place, do you?"

9

WHEN THE GROUP STEPPED BACK THROUGH the mirror, Sabrina suddenly felt her massive size. Being an eight-foot-tall, twelve-hundred-pound grizzly bear made the regular-sized room feel much smaller.

"I'll never get through the doorway," Sabrina worried.

"You won't have to," Jack said as he stepped through the reflection. "Just click those heels together and you'll go anywhere you want. But before you do, you'll need these."

Jack held three walkie-talkies. He opened Momma Bear's handbag and stuffed one inside, then slid open a panel in Daphne's tin torso and popped in another. He kept the third for himself.

"These will help you keep in touch with me."

"You're not going in with us?" Sabrina asked.

"Are you kidding?" Jack cried. "I'm on Ferryport Landing's Most Wanted list by now. Even if I disguised myself, Charming is sure to have security that can sniff me out. I can't take the chance.

I'm going to stand outside the mansion and direct you. When you find the map of Charming's next target, we'll go save your grandmother and Canis."

"OK," Sabrina said, looking down at the slippers on her huge furry feet. "I just click them together?" she asked, feeling ridiculous.

"Three times," Daphne cheerfully reminded her.

"'There's no place like Charming's mansion?'"

Jack nodded in agreement. Daphne put her hand on Sabrina's arm and held on tightly. Jack reached over and did the same.

"There's no place like Charming's mansion. There's no place like Charming's mansion. There's no place like Charming's mansion."

The last thing Sabrina saw was Elvis trotting into the room. In his mouth was a piece of fabric Granny claimed was from a giant's pants, as well as a big scrap of Jack's pants. He spit them out on the floor and whined for attention, but suddenly there was a pop and the lights went out. Sabrina's ears filled with a squeaky sound, like someone was slowly releasing the air from a balloon, and when the lights came back on, the three of them were standing in front of Charming's mansion.

Marble columns framed a golden front door with a coat of arms above it, depicting a lion fighting a snake. The lawn was immaculately trimmed and bordered by stone paths and clipped shrubbery. A statue of Prince Charming surrounded by admiring woodland animals rose out of a fountain in the middle of the lawn. Several hulking attendants with green skin and oversized muscles—parking valets—waited by the circular driveway, opening car doors, taking keys, and driving the cars away.

A car pulled up in front of the house, and a blond woman in a blue bonnet and a puffy dress got out. She reached into the backseat for a long white staff with a curled end. Before the attendant could close the door for her, half a dozen sheep tumbled out and eagerly followed the woman inside.

"Little Bo Peep!" Daphne cried. "Can you believe it?"

"OK, girls, I'm going to stay out here and let you know if the cops show up. Keep your radios on and try to stay inconspicuous," Jack said.

"I'm a grizzly bear in a dress," Sabrina muttered.

"Charming's office is on the second floor," Jack continued. "I'd mingle with the guests for a while, work the crowd, and find your way up there without attracting attention. Once you find the map, pop yourselves back down here and we'll go find your giant," Jack finished. He gave them a thumbs-up and disappeared into some nearby trees.

"He makes it sound so simple," Sabrina grumbled to Daphne.

A line of guests waited to be announced, so the girls walked to the back of it. In front of them were a large man and his wife, having some kind of argument.

"Isn't there a line for the rich people?" the woman groaned.

"Maybe if we'd gotten here earlier, we'd be inside already," the man grunted. His voice was slurred, and Sabrina thought he might be drunk.

"I wanted to look nice for the ball," the woman said defensively.

"You wanted to look nice for the prince," he muttered.

"Are you going to harp on that again?" The woman sighed.

She turned and noticed Sabrina and Daphne. Her cheeks flushed red, and she forced a sheepish smile to her face. Even in her embarrassment, the woman was radiant. Her beautiful amber hair cascaded in curls down her neck and her bright green eyes sparkled in the light, competing for brilliance with her pearly white smile.

"Good evening," she said politely.

Her husband turned to see who she was speaking to, and the agony of his face was revealed. His features were pushed flat, giving him a catlike appearance, accentuated by the mane of hair that framed his face. Long fangs crept out of his mouth and hung down nearly to his chin. But his most horrible feature was his eyes, bright yellow slits that blinked at them fiercely. Sabrina knew exactly who they were—Beauty and the Beast.

"Good evening," the Beast grunted. "Nice to see you, Woodsman. How on earth did you and Momma Bear come to be acquainted?"

The girls weren't prepared for questions and stood dumbfounded.

"You're such a gossip," Beauty scolded. "What Poppa Bear doesn't know won't hurt him."

Several more guests joined the line. Sabrina turned around to see a small white rabbit in a vest clutching an old-fashioned chain watch in his paw. He looked at the time and stuffed the watch into his pocket.

"For once, we are not late," he said to his companions, three mice wearing black sunglasses and carrying canes.

"Always the worrywart," one of the mice said as he tapped his cane against the ground.

"I told you we would make it," the second added.

"All that worrying about time is going to give you a heart attack," the third mouse concluded.

"I believe in being punctual," the White Rabbit said defensively.

"Have you heard the news?" the second mouse squeaked to the crowd.

"No, I want to tell. I heard it first," the first mouse cried. "Relda Grimm has been carried off by a giant!"

The folks in line gasped in surprise and turned their attention to the little mouse.

"Are you sure?" the Beast asked.

"Maybe you'd prefer an eyewitness," the first mouse cried. "I may be blind, but my hearing is just fine."

The Beast rolled his eyes.

"A giant? That's impossible," Beauty exclaimed.

"I didn't believe it, either, but it's true," the White Rabbit replied. "The giant has been stomping around all over town scaring the humans to death. The Three are working overtime, showering the town in forgetful dust. Be prepared to dig deep, my friends. The damage is extensive, and forgetful dust costs a pretty penny. You know Charming's going to ask us to foot the bill."

Sabrina hung on every word.

"If she's dead, we might actually be able to leave Ferryport Landing!" Beauty cried, unable to hide her excitement. "Has anyone tried?"

"The barrier is still intact," said the third mouse, almost stumbling over a pebble as he stepped forward with the moving line. "We tried it this morning."

"Well, I wouldn't get your hopes up about Relda meeting an untimely demise," the White Rabbit said. "I'm sure Canis will save her. He always does."

"Oh, that's not going to be a problem this time," the third mouse chirped. "The giant carried him away, too!"

"Two birds with one very big stone," the second mouse sang with glee.

"So it's just a matter of time," the Beast said.

"Maybe not," the second mouse said. "I hear they've found the granddaughters."

Everyone groaned.

"I thought they were dead!" Beauty said.

"No, just missing. Apparently, whoever kidnapped their parents didn't get them," the White Rabbit said.

"I'm sorry," Sabrina interrupted, "but did you say that the girls' parents have been kidnapped?"

"The family thinks they abandoned them, but I've heard whispers that Henry and his wife were abducted," the Beast answered.

Sabrina and Daphne shared a stunned look.

"But it gets better!" the first mouse said.

"Indeed?" Beauty asked.

"I hear they're already trying to rescue their grandmother. Can you believe it?" said the White Rabbit.

"That's the dumbest thing I've ever heard, and when it comes to the Grimms, that's saying something," the Beast said. "Two kids taking on a giant? The whole family will be pushing up daisies by morning."

The crowd laughed.

"Momma Bear, you must be so excited," Beauty said, taking Sabrina's heavy paws in her delicate hands. "Soon you'll be reunited with your family. Are they still hiding out in that Romanian zoo?"

"Uh . . . yes, that will be wonderful," Sabrina muttered, doing her best not to swat Beauty across the yard and then stomp the rest of them into paste.

"Do you know who kidnapped my—I mean, their—parents?" said Sabrina.

"Word is it was the Scarlet Hand," the White Rabbit replied.

"Who?" Daphne asked.

"You people are horrible," a voice said from behind them. Sabrina turned and saw a lovely brown-skinned woman with dazzling green eyes. She wore a diamond tiara and a beautiful evening gown. She looked at the group with shock and disgust.

"Briar Rose," Beauty said nervously. "I think you may have stepped into the middle of a conversation and misheard something."

"I heard all I need to hear," Briar Rose said.

The crowd shifted uncomfortably and turned away from her accusing stare while Sabrina's mind filled with possibilities. Could it be true? Their parents hadn't abandoned them? Could someone have kidnapped them?

Soon Sabrina and Daphne were almost at the front of the line. Mr. Seven stood at the door, this time without his pointy I AM AN IDIOT hat. He announced Beauty and the Beast, and the couple disappeared into the hum of the party.

"Good evening," Mr. Seven said as he opened the door for them. He cupped his hands together and yelled, "Momma Bear, escorted this evening by the Tin Woodsman," as the girls entered the room.

The mansion was a spectacular display of wealth and taste. A crystal chandelier hung from the ceiling, and a beautiful red-carpeted staircase led up to a large landing where four musicians played violins. The room was already crowded with people, animals, and monsters of all shapes and sizes—Everafters as far as the eye could see. They wandered around, talking and drinking champagne. Some laughed at jokes while others argued politics. A very ugly couple of trolls dressed in evening wear danced to the music, and several hulking waiters hurried around the room, extending trays of appetizers to guests. No one seemed to be bothered that there were ogres and winged people hobnobbing with talking animals, so Sabrina's worries that people would notice a man made of metal and a bear in a polka-dotted dress quickly dissolved.

"Sabrina, all of the Everafters wish we were dead," Daphne said.

Sabrina looked around the room. Every fairy-tale creature she had ever read about seemed to be there: the Mad Hatter, Mowgli and Baloo, Briar Rose—even Geppetto was off in a corner chatting with Ali Baba. And Sabrina knew they all hated the Grimms. As unsettling as it was, she could understand why. Even though Ms. Smirt had dumped the girls into some awful foster homes, Sabrina and Daphne knew they could always run away. For the Everafters there was no escape, and it had been that way

for almost two hundred years. *It must be torment for them*, she thought.

"Let's get out of here as soon as we can," Sabrina said.

"Good idea. Where should we start?" Daphne asked.

"We need to get into the mayor's office, but we also need to know where Charming is while we're doing it," Sabrina explained.

Daphne looked around the room but couldn't spot him.

"Let's just stay out of the way and keep our ears open. Once we know where he is, we'll make our way upstairs. For now, let's mingle."

The two walked awkwardly around the main room, gawking at the various literary celebrities and capturing bits of conversations.

"So she's not coming?" a lion asked a huge black panther. The panther licked its paw and hungrily eyed Sabrina.

"She never comes," the panther said. "If *I* had left him at the altar, the last place I'd want to go is the man's house. I think it's very respectful of Snow White not to show her face here."

"But that was almost four hundred years ago. The man has been married at least half a dozen times since," the lion said. "Cinderella, Briar Rose, and Rapunzel are all here. If they can move on, then Snow White surely can. This community is important."

At that moment Mr. Seven shouted from the top of the red staircase, "Ladies and gentlemen, we're pleased that you could attend Ferryport Landing's one hundredth annual community ball!"

The musicians laid down their instruments and everyone turned their attention to the mayor's assistant.

"Allow me to introduce your host for this evening. Your mayor, His Majesty, Prince Charming."

The violinists immediately broke into a stately song as a pair of double doors at the top of the stairs swung open. The crowd burst into applause as Charming waved and descended the staircase.

He glided around the room, shook hands with everyone he met, kissed women on the hands, and called everyone by name. Mr. Seven followed closely, handing out business cards.

"What do you say, Woodsman?" Charming asked, taking Daphne's hand and shaking it vigorously.

"Hello," Daphne seethed, unable to hide her contempt.

Charming reached over, took Sabrina's massive hairy paw, and placed a kiss on it. "Momma Bear, as lovely as ever," he said with a wink. "I hope the two of you are having a wonderful time."

"We are, thank you," Sabrina said sharply. Maybe she had gained a bit of Momma Bear's aggressiveness with the disguise, because for the second time that night she thought she might like to swat someone with her paw. One quick whack and she could probably take Charming's head clean off his shoulders. Instead, she smiled and did her best to curtsy, imagining how ridiculous this move looked from a twelve-hundred-pound bear.

"Please eat, drink, have a wonderful time. This celebration is for us," Charming said as he swept on to the center of the room.

"Friends, I am so happy that you could all attend the annual ball," he continued. "Each year we gather together as a community to toast our hard work and, most importantly, our patience."

Charming's words sent a frustrated rumble through the crowd.

"But once again, your support is needed to continue to build our community," he said. "There is still work to be done, and we need your help to maintain services, to fund our fine police force, and to support various other community endeavors. So I ask you, when you contribute tonight, give deeply. In fact, give until it hurts, or I'll put you all in jail!"

For a moment there was complete silence, and then Charming grinned boyishly. The crowd burst into nervous laughter.

Suddenly a woman pushed through the crowd. Her face was white with powder, as was the long wig she wore on her head. An overly generous black pencil had been used to accentuate eyebrows she didn't have, and to draw a large black mole on her left cheek. She wore a royal gown, decorated with large red hearts, and flanking her on either side stood two armed guards who, much to the girls' amazement, were playing cards as tall as men.

"Prince Charming, what are you doing about the giant?" the woman demanded. The crowd grew silent, but Charming merely smiled at her.

"Your Majesty. It is such an honor to have the Queen of Hearts here at the gala," he said.

"You haven't answered my question," the queen snapped, eyeing the crowd to make sure everyone was paying attention. "I think the community deserves to know what you are doing to protect this town and if the money we give each year at this party of yours is well spent."

"Every Everafter can rest assured that my administration is on top of the problem," the prince said. "The sheriff and his deputies have been searching the forests, and I have my best witches busy casting locator spells. And if that doesn't work, well, I'll just go lock up the next two-hundred-foot man I see."

The crowd chuckled at his joke.

"That's all fine and good, Charming," the queen replied. "But one must ask how a giant got loose in the first place. This kind of thing would never have happened in Wonderland. When I was ruler, people knew better than to try such shenanigans. You have to be firm with the criminal element."

Some of the crowd muttered in agreement, but Charming only smiled wider.

"Well, Your Majesty, let's not go losing our heads over this," he said. The crowd exploded with laughter, causing the Queen of Hearts to turn red with rage. "It's just one giant, and—"

"I've heard a rumor that you are actually controlling this

giant," Sabrina said, hardly believing that the words came from her mouth.

"Momma Bear, I never pegged you for a gossip," the prince replied. "Did this nasty little rumor you heard carry more information? For instance, why I would want a giant smashing up the town?"

"So you could buy the land back cheap and rebuild your kingdom," Sabrina replied.

Charming's face turned pale. "Nonsense," he muttered.

"What if the Grimms hear of this?" asked the Queen of Hearts.

"Relda is already aware of it. The giant has carried her off," the prince informed her.

The crowd roared in shock.

"Relda Grimm is in the hands of a giant?" the queen cried.

"As is Mr. Canis," Charming added.

The crowd went silent, and then a smattering of applause broke out. Many of the Everafters shook hands and patted one another on the back, while others looked worried and upset.

"Canis will finally get what's coming to him," a troll said, giving a cheer.

"Take that back!" Daphne screamed.

Sabrina tried to pinch her to be quiet, but her paws slid off her sister's tin body.

"People! Unfortunately, this celebration is turning into a town hall meeting," Charming called above the noise. "If you have any further concerns, I want you to know that my door is always open . . . between the hours of eight and eight fifteen every morning. Please call for an appointment. For now, let's dance, drink, be merry, and most of all, be ourselves, free of the disguises we wear to fit into this pathetic, boring little town. The night is young, and by the grace of magic, so are we."

Charming's words were followed by another lively tune from the violinists, and the festive mood soon returned.

The girls mingled in the crowd, barely able to contain themselves when they heard angry, threatening words about their family from the mouths of characters they grew up loving. It seemed that the only topic of conversation of the evening was how wonderful the world would be if the Grimm family dropped off the face of the Earth. By the time the clock struck eight forty-five, both girls had heard enough.

"We have to get upstairs," Sabrina said to Daphne. "If we stick around here any longer, we're going to change back, and these people will probably kill us. I'll search Charming's office. You stay here and be a lookout. Find somewhere out of the way and warn me on the walkie-talkie if he's coming."

"Good luck," Daphne said, wrapping her hard metal arms around Sabrina and hugging her.

Sabrina navigated through the crowd. As she approached the

steps, she thought she'd finally found her opportunity. At least until Sheriff Hamstead stepped in her way.

"Young lady, you are under arrest," Hamstead said.

Sabrina wondered what she should do. She could probably knock the sheriff down with one swing of her big bear paw, but everyone would see. Running away didn't seem like an option, either.

"For being the prettiest lady at the ball," the sheriff continued.

"Uh, thank you," she stammered, somewhat confused.

"Wonderful party, don't you think?" said Hamstead as he transformed into his true pig self.

"Yes," she said. "Could you excuse me? I have to visit the ladies' room."

Hamstead apologized and let her pass. Sabrina lumbered up the stairs until she reached the top. She walked past the musicians and down a long hallway. Once she was out of sight of the crowd, she made sure no one was following, then reached into her purse and pulled out the walkie-talkie, awkwardly switching it on with her big paws.

"Jack, I'm upstairs," she said.

"Good job, duck. His office is the last one—" Jack said, his voice popping and crackling.

"I can barely hear you. Say again," Sabrina said.

"It's the last one on the right!" Jack repeated, still sounding distant.

Sabrina walked down the hallway. When she got to the end, she found the door Jack had described. She opened it, and standing before her was another grizzly bear ready to pounce. She nearly screamed, but the bear did nothing. In fact, it didn't even twitch. Sabrina realized it was stuffed. Beyond it was a room dedicated to Prince Charming's hunting trophies. Several mounted deer heads, a stuffed fox, and a wild boar overlooked the mayor's immense desk. A rattlesnake sat on top of it, poised and ready to strike. What portions of the walls weren't covered in dead animals were hung with portraits of the prince done in various artistic styles. There was even an abstract portrait in which his nose was on his forehead.

"Classy," Sabrina whispered to herself. She reached for her walkie-talkie and pushed the button. "I'm in."

"The coast is clear down here," Daphne's voice said. "Charming is busy talking to a raccoon in a tuxedo. That's so crazy!"

"Look for a map or something like that," Jack's voice squawked through the radio. "Charming keeps records of everything."

Dozens of files and reports littered the top of the mayor's desk, including an unfolded map of the town. Certain areas were circled in red with the words *reported sightings* scrawled next to them.

"Jack, are you there?" Sabrina said into the walkie-talkie.

"Yes," his voice crackled.

"I found a map with some circles on it, but there's nothing that says the exact time or location of a meeting. In fact, to me it looks like Charming's trying to track the giant as well."

"I doubt it . . . that . . . homes . . . too." Jack's voice broke up.

"Jack, I can't hear you. Try to get closer," Sabrina said, but there was no response.

"Daphne, I've lost Jack somehow. I'm going to take the map. What is Charming doing?" Sabrina asked. But there was no response from her sister, either.

She looked around the room. In the corner was a television. Hooked to the back by a cord was a video camera, and on the television's screen was a frozen image of the Applebee farm. She crossed the room and found the remote control. She picked it up awkwardly and after several difficult seconds managed to get her giant paw to press the play button.

The screen came to life with the most amazing scene. A giant beanstalk was exploding upward from the ground, soaring high into the sky and disappearing off the top edge of the TV. Within seconds, an enormous body came crawling down it, and the sight sent shivers through Sabrina. It stomped down on the little Applebee farmhouse just as Mr. Applebee leaped out the door. Granny had been right. The lens cap did mean that someone—Charming—had taped the whole violent episode!

"Daphne, I found a tape in Charming's office that shows the

giant destroying the farmhouse. Now we have proof that he and the giant are working together," Sabrina said.

But before she could finish her sentence, the door burst open and the Tin Woodsman was pushed inside. Behind her was Charming, looking murderous. He slammed the door and took a crossbow from the wall, where it was hanging like a piece of art.

"I'm sorry," Daphne said. "He snuck up on me before I could warn you."

"Who are you?" he demanded.

"I'm Momma Bear," Sabrina lied.

"Is that so?" Charming sneered. "That would be interesting, since it's almost December and you should be three weeks into your hibernation by now."

"I—I—I didn't want to miss such a lovely party," Sabrina stammered.

Next to the door sat a quiver of arrows. Charming selected one, inserted it in the crossbow, and pulled the bowstring back. Then he aimed it at Sabrina's heart.

"I'm going to give you until the count of five to tell me who you are, or your head is going to join the others on my wall," he threatened coolly. "I'm not playing any more games with you people. I've told you already I'm not interested in joining the Scarlet Hand. Your revolution is not for me. One!"

Sabrina looked over at the clock. There were only seconds left before the magic would wear off, but more than the five Charming had promised them.

"We're Relda Grimm's granddaughters," she blurted out desperately.

"Two."

"We used a magic wand to change our shape so we could sneak into your house," Daphne cried. Oily tears leaked from her eyes.

"Three."

"We're not part of any revolution!" Sabrina insisted. "We just want our grandmother back!"

"Four."

"We're not lying to you!" Daphne sobbed.

"Five."

Sabrina closed her eyes tightly and awaited her death, wondering if she would be stuffed like the other bear in Charming's office or if her body would change back after her heart stopped beating. But when nothing happened, she bravely opened her eyes. She and her sister had magically morphed back into their normal bodies.

"Ladies, you are in a lot of trouble," Charming said, removing the arrow from his crossbow. "You've used a magical item to help a known criminal escape from jail, infiltrated an Everafters party without an invitation, impersonated Everafters, committed espionage against a government official, broken into my home, put the Ferryport Landing Fund-raising Ball in serious jeopardy, and destroyed two pairs of Sheriff Hamstead's pants."

"We didn't ruin your stupid party," Sabrina argued.

"I've got to get you out of here. If that crowd downstairs sees the two of you, the top of this house will blow off," Charming replied. "Hamstead can toss you in some old sacks and carry you out the servants' entrance. He can take you down to the jailhouse and let you cool off in a cell."

Sabrina made a grab for the video camera. The cord came with it, and the image of the giant faded from the television screen.

"We're not going anywhere without our grandmother and Mr. Canis," Sabrina said. "This tape is all the evidence we need. How do you think those people downstairs are going to feel knowing you are working with a giant and intend to buy up this town?"

Sabrina expected Charming to fight for the tape, but instead he only laughed. "You're just like your parents." Charming chuckled. "Henry was always shooting his mouth off before his brain could catch up, and Veronica was the suspicious one. What an unsettling combination you are."

"You knew our parents?" Daphne said. She leaned against the bookcase, and Sabrina heard a *click*. At once, all the portraits of Charming flipped over revealing paintings of Snow White. In some of the paintings, Charming and Snow looked lovingly into each other's eyes. In others, they were holding hands in a field of poppies. Some just featured the teacher, looking angelic in the sunshine.

Charming looked up at the paintings and seemed almost pained by them. He stomped across the room, shoved Daphne aside, and clicked the button she had activated. All the paintings flipped again.

"You two are never to tell—" he started, but something moved in the window that cut him off. "Did you see that?"

"See what?" Sabrina asked.

"ENGLISHMAN!" a booming voice growled, shaking the windows in their frames, and then a giant, pus-filled eye peered into the house.

"Looks like your business partner is here," Sabrina said.

Charming calmly picked up the phone on his desk and dialed a number. "Mr. Seven, are you aware that there is a giant outside?" he said into the receiver, as if he were informing a waiter that there was a hair in his soup. "Well, now you do . . . No, this isn't some kind of emergency drill . . . Well, I agree, we should do something about it before the guests panic. Maybe you should send the witches out to put a protection spell on the house . . . Well, of course it's a good idea!"

Charming slammed the phone down, crossed the room, and roughly dragged both girls out of his office and down the hall.

"Where are you taking us?" Sabrina demanded.

"Outside," the prince said. "You wanted to find your grandmother. Well, her ride just showed up."

An acidic fear rose up in Sabrina's throat as they stumbled along in the prince's grasp. "You can't take us out there with that thing!" Sabrina cried, pulling at Charming's iron grip.

"HELP!" Daphne shouted as they turned a corner and headed down a long hall toward the back of the house. Sabrina joined her, and together they drew the attention of the guests.

"Those are the Grimm children!" a goose squawked angrily.

"I have the situation under control," said Charming with his toothy smile.

"They're spying on us!" the Queen of Hearts gasped. "Off with their—"

"They aren't spies, my friends," the prince said as he changed course and pulled the girls down the stairs with him into the angry crowd. "Please, go back to the celebration. There are waiters circulating with finger foods and—"

But before he could get the words out of his mouth a horrible crunching sound filled Sabrina's ears. The partygoers looked to the ceiling, only to see it ripped away right before their eyes. Pieces of plaster rained down, and a collective scream erupted among the Everafters.

"The sky is falling! The sky is falling!" a tiny chicken cried as it raced for the door, only to get caught in a stampede of terror when the hole in the roof was replaced by the giant's horrible, gnarled face, breathing his rancid, rotten-egg breath down on the crowd.

The Queen of Hearts ran to a nearby window, threw open the curtains, and tried to climb out. Her playing card attendants rushed over in time to keep her from falling. The rest of the crowd ran in all directions, and the panic gave Sabrina and Daphne a chance to break Charming's grip. They rushed into the crowd and ducked between legs and feathers as all sorts of unusual creatures rushed around them.

"Where is the murderer?" the giant bellowed.

"He's not here, big boy. The murderer is not here!" Charming shouted as he turned to face the monster.

"Liars! You protect him," the giant growled. "I smell his murderous blood. He released me in hopes of killing me, but my fate will not be like that of my brothers and sisters. He is here, and I will have him."

Charming looked up the staircase to the violinists, who were scattered in fear. "I didn't tell you to stop playing," he said, snapping his fingers at them. Bewildered, the musicians went back to their overturned chairs, set them upright, and continued their concert as if a giant weren't staring down at them.

"Fe, fi, fo, fum, I smell the blood of an—"

"I think we've all had enough of your temper tantrum," Charming interrupted.

Suddenly three figures fluttered into the air and hovered around the giant's head. One of them was an ugly old woman on a broom; the second was a striking beauty dressed all in black, who levitated off the ground; and the third was a blond lady inside a silver bubble. As she floated by, Sabrina recognized her as Glinda from the hospital. All three held magic wands they waved threateningly at the giant. The monster swatted at the witches, but they weaved and bobbed away from his massive hand. The ugly witch waved her wand, and a rocket of flame shot out of it and exploded on the giant's chest, searing his shirt and causing him to scream in agony.

"Stop!" Daphne cried. "Our family is in his pocket!" The little girl broke away from her sister and ran outside. Sabrina, followed by Charming, rushed after her.

The witches continued their assault.

"Leave while you can, giant!" Charming shouted.

The second witch raised her wand and fired a bolt of lightning, hitting the giant in the face. The giant bellowed. A charred black smear had joined the other ugly features on his gruesome face.

Glinda waved her wand, and a spray of ice froze the giant's backside and spread to cover the rest of his body. Within seconds, the massive man was encased in ice, but soon cracks appeared and, with flexing muscles and a powerful roar, the giant broke free. Enormous chunks of ice rained down on the driveway, flattening an unlucky car.

The doors of the mansion were thrown wide, and a dozen men rushed past the girls. Each wore a purple tunic embroidered with a red lion on the chest. At the front of the attack was a man Sabrina instinctively knew to be King Arthur. The knights thrust their swords into the air, then attacked the giant's feet, whacking angrily at an exposed big toe. The giant bellowed and stomped angrily, trying to squash his attackers. Each of the men was lightning quick and dodged the giant's heels, managing to strike at his exposed ankle in the process. Shrieking in pain, the giant quickly turned and fled.

Charming bowed in respect as the king and his knights turned to face him.

"I am indebted to the Knights of the Round Table. Thank you, Your Highness," Charming said.

"Your thanks will not be enough, Charming," King Arthur barked. "The beast destroyed my car. Trust that you will find a repair estimate in the mail this week."

Charming scowled, but as the party guests filed out of the half-destroyed mansion, he forced a smile. Mr. Seven rushed to the prince's side, carrying a large black pot he held out to the approaching crowd.

"Friends," said Charming, back in his gracious-host mode, "who says nothing exciting ever happens in Ferryport Landing?" He chuckled. But this time his wit and charm fell on angry ears.

"Is this what we're paying you for?" the White Rabbit said as he hopped past.

"People, there's no need to leave," Charming said. "We'll have the mansion back to its old self in just a matter of moments. There's plenty of food and drink, and we've even arranged a door prize."

"As the elected leader of this community, I would have thought you'd take the safety of your constituents much more seriously," a Bengal tiger said as he stalked past.

"I assure you, Shere Khan—"

But the tiger didn't stop to hear Charming's assurances.

"Well, if you all must go, please don't forget to donate to the Ferryport Community Fund," the prince continued, kicking Mr. Seven, who immediately held the pot higher so that everyone could see.

"I do believe this town is in need of some new leadership," the Queen of Hearts said as she left. Charming said nothing as he watched the last of his guests drive away.

"Put the pot down, Mr. Seven," he said. The dwarf slowly lowered the empty pot and took a peek inside. It was completely empty.

"We want our grandmother and her friend," Sabrina demanded.

"This is all your fault!" Charming shouted as he turned on the girls.

"What?"

"You two brought him here."

"If you can't control your giant, then maybe you shouldn't be working with one," Daphne advised.

"I'm not working with any giant. Only a fool would make a deal with a giant," Charming said.

"That's a lie!" Sabrina yelled. "He's one of your goons, just like those guys you met at the cabin."

"Ladies, I am nobility. I don't have goons. Those men didn't work for me. I was there to arrest them and their boss."

"Well, if you're not their boss, who is?" Sabrina demanded.

Charming snatched the video camera from Sabrina's hand. He opened a side panel where a small LCD screen folded out. Then he rewound the recording, pressed the play button, and handed the camera back to the girls. The image was shaky at first, but then suddenly it cleared up as the person holding the camera set it down on the hill that overlooked Applebee's farm. Four men were talking to one another. Two of them were extremely tall, another was short and fat, and the fourth couldn't be seen. It was obvious who the three visible ones were—Bobby, Tony, and Steve—the goons who had attacked the family at the hospital. Finally, the fourth figure stepped in front of the lens, leaned down, and grinned broadly. It was Jack.

"This tape is evidence we found on Jack when he was arrested.

He wanted a record of himself killing a giant," Charming said. "I presume he intended to upload it to the Internet so everyone could see."

Jack laughed wildly at the camera, held up a small white bean, and then rushed down the hill. Soon the familiar footage of the beanstalk and the destruction by the giant played again.

"So you're not trying to buy up the town to rebuild your kingdom?" Daphne asked.

"Oh, I *am* trying to buy up this town," Charming said. "But there are better ways to get what you want than to let a giant loose on the countryside."

Sabrina didn't know whether to be furious at his admission or respect his honesty.

"Why did you send the sheriff after us?" Daphne asked.

"He was supposed to pick you up and take you somewhere safe until we could hunt down the giant and find your grandmother," Charming said.

"Every Everafter in this town wishes we were dead," Sabrina said. "Why would you want to help us?"

"I have my reasons."

"I'm confused," Daphne said. "Why would Jack bring us here and tell us this story about you being the bad guy?"

"Because, if he kept you busy, he could go back to your house," the prince said.

"But he can't get in. He doesn't have the keys," Sabrina replied.

"He doesn't need the keys," Daphne said with a gasp. "We didn't say 'good-bye' to the house when we left. We used the slippers. The house is unlocked."

Hamstead, in his human form, came rushing out of the mansion.

"I've got the deputies chasing the giant," he said. "He's heading into the woods in the direction of Widow's Peak."

"Good work, Sheriff," Charming said.

"We've also searched the grounds. Jack's gone," Hamstead continued, "but he left this to lure the giant." He held out a bloody handkerchief.

"Join your men, Sheriff. The girls and I will call you if we need you," Charming ordered.

"Where are you going, sir?" Hamstead asked.

The prince took Sabrina's arm and urged Daphne to take the other. "We're going to the Grimm house. I have an unsettling notion of what our giant killer is up to," Charming said.

Sabrina clicked her heels together.

"There's no place like home. There's no place like home. There's no place like home."

Instantly, the girls and Charming were standing outside of Granny's house. The front door was wide open, and through the doorway they could see that Jack had ransacked it. They tentatively walked inside and found bookshelves tipped over, furniture overturned, and even the couch cushions thrown aside. Jack had torn though kitchen cupboards, emptied closets, and destroyed antiques. Sabrina couldn't help but burn with embarrassment. Jack had tricked her. She was supposed to be street-smart and savvy. She was the one who was supposed to pull fast ones on everyone else. She thought of herself as the queen of the sneaks, and now she was a sucker.

"Elvis!" Daphne cried suddenly. The giant dog was nowhere to be seen. Daphne shouted his name, and after several painful moments of silence, a low bark could be heard from upstairs. Daphne rushed up the steps, followed by Sabrina and Charming. She threw open the door to Mirror's room and found Elvis lying on the floor in a small puddle of his own blood. He had a serious cut on his belly, yet he barked happily when he saw the girls. Daphne knelt down and kissed the dog gently on his nose. When she lifted her face, tears were pouring down her cheeks.

"He hurt Elvis," the little girl sobbed.

"Girls, we have to find Jack," Charming said coldly. "We don't have time for this mongrel."

Sabrina and Daphne looked at the man as if he were a moldy sandwich slowly turning to soup in the bottom of the refrigerator. The prince groaned and took his cell phone from his pocket. He dialed a number and sighed impatiently.

"Mr. Seven, I need you to send one of the Three to the Grimm house. The door is open. There's a dog that needs medical assistance . . . Yes, a dog . . . a D-O-G. No, Mr. Seven, I don't know what's wrong with him, maybe a broken rib . . . No, Mr. Seven . . . Yes, Mr. Seven . . . Mr. Seven, if you don't stop asking me questions, I'm going to feed you to this dog."

Sabrina eyed the man suspiciously, and Charming caught her gaze. "And, Mr. Seven, my orders are that whichever one of the witches comes, she will respect this house," Charming added. "No snooping."

Daphne wrapped her arms around the prince's neck and hugged him as he hung up his phone.

"Thank you," she sobbed, and for a brief moment Charming seemed to enjoy the hug, but then he pulled away from her.

"You're ruining my suit," he replied, wiping his lapel clean of the girl's tears. "Where is the mirror's guardian?"

Sabrina gazed into the reflection. Mirror was missing.

"Mirror!" Charming shouted. "Your assistance is required!"

"You have to step through it," said Sabrina.

"I'm aware of how it works," the prince said impatiently. "I used to be engaged to one of its former owners."

He stepped into the reflection and disappeared. Sabrina followed closely behind, leaving Daphne to nurse Elvis.

Mirror was lying on his side on the cold marble floor, barely conscious and covered in bruises. Charming knelt down to him and lifted the pudgy man's head. Mirror slowly opened his eyes and grimaced in pain.

"He was too strong and fast for me. I couldn't stop him," Mirror groaned.

"What did he take?" Charming asked.

"I tried to fight him off, but he just laughed at me," Mirror complained.

"Focus, man! We need to know if Jack took anything."

"He took the beans," Mirror replied.

"The beans?" Charming said.

"The magic beans. He took the whole jar," Mirror whimpered.

"How? He doesn't have a key," Sabrina asked, reaching into her pocket and pulling out Granny's key ring.

"I forgot to remind you to lock the door after you let him take a peek," said the little man.

"I don't get it," Sabrina said. "If killing the giant will make him famous again, what does he want with the beans?"

"It's insurance. If his fame starts to fade, he'll let another giant out with another one of those beans. The giant will kill people and destroy things, and then Jack will come to the rescue," Charming explained.

"But how is he going to find the giant again?" Sabrina asked. "We haven't been able to, and he's two hundred feet tall."

"He's not going to have to find it—it's going to find him," Charming answered. "Giants have a great sense of smell, especially when it comes to blood. That's why the giant showed up at the mansion. Jack's fat lip was all the giant needed to get a whiff of his blood. It's my own stupid mistake, really. I shouldn't have slugged him. I fell right into his plan as well. It's amazing, really, that they can smell anything over their own stink. If one touches you, you can't wash off the odor for weeks."

Suddenly Sabrina thought of the two pieces of fabric that Elvis had brought into the room just before the group left for Charming's mansion. One was Granny Relda's cloth from the giant; the other was a piece of Jack's pants. Elvis had been trying to warn them that Jack had been near a giant, Sabrina realized. She was a terrible detective—she couldn't recognize a clue when a two-hundred-pound Great Dane offered it to her. She wanted to kick herself, but she needed to focus on what Charming had said.

"But if giants have such great noses, why didn't this one attack us here? Jack was in our house for hours," she said to Charming.

"Protection spells. If Relda is anything, she's careful. We have one on the jailhouse, too," he replied.

"So how are we going to stop him?"

"Mirror, I'm going to need something," Charming said.

ಌ

Sabrina unlocked the door labeled MAGICAL ARMORY and let the prince inside. The room was filled with all types of weapons—bows and arrows, swords, a nasty-looking pole with a spiky metal ball attached by a chain, and hundreds of other sharp objects. Some things were obviously magical, as they glowed or hummed, while most just shone with horrible possibilities.

Charming pointed to a sword on the wall. "That's the one," he said.

Mirror hobbled into the room with a worried face. "I find this very unwise. There is already one Everafter running around with magic; this town does not need a second. Especially with Excalibur. Any person whose skin is pierced by its blade is a goner. Even the tiniest scratch will kill you."

Sabrina took the sword off the wall and held it in her hand. It was long and wide, with a jewel-encrusted handle. An odd tingle raced through her when she held it with both hands. She felt powerful, the way King Arthur must have felt when Excalibur belonged to him.

"Sabrina, is this someone you can trust?" Mirror asked as he gestured to the mayor.

"No, he's not," she said. "I've heard what this town thinks of my family and what my death might mean for their freedom. How do I know you won't just stab me in the back when I'm not looking?"

"Grimm, I am not your friend," Charming said. "I resent your family for the life they have forced me to live for the last two hundred years, and I resent you for the future that you represent. I'm not doing this for you. I'm doing it for me. As much as Baba Yaga's spell has trapped me in Ferryport Landing, it has also benefited me. I have power here. I have wealth and respect. If Jack shows the world that giants and fairy tales are real, then life in this town will change, and my position as its ruler—I mean, mayor—might be challenged. Therefore, you and I are in an unusual situation. Tonight, it is in my best interest to be your ally, and I will help you save your grandmother and Canis. If that is the only solution, then so be it. But rest assured, Grimm, tomorrow I am your enemy again."

Sabrina looked up into Charming's eyes and saw that he was being honest, even if his brand of honesty made her sick to her stomach. Oddly enough, she trusted him. She set the sword down and reached into her pocket. She took out the picture of her family, and gazed at their faces—her mother and father, Mr. Canis, and finally, Granny Relda. She had to do something to get the old woman back. She wasn't going to lose her family all over again. She took up the heavy sword again and handed it to the prince.

Mirror continued to protest, limping along, as Charming and Sabrina exited the room and returned through the mirror. Daphne was waiting for them with Elvis. They gently carried the dog into the hallway, and then Sabrina carefully locked the door to Mirror's room.

"You stay here with Elvis," Sabrina ordered her sister.

"No way!" Daphne cried. "We're Grimms; this is what *we* do!"

"This is dangerous."

"Whatever," the little girl said, grabbing Sabrina's hand tightly.

Sabrina surrendered, hooked her finger into Charming's pocket, and clicked Dorothy's shoes together. "There's no place like where Jack is hiding now," she began.

"Wait, Sabrina, wouldn't these shoes take us to wherever Mom and Dad are?" Daphne wondered aloud.

Sabrina's eyes grew wide with possibility.

"We can save them next," her sister said happily.

Sabrina couldn't let herself hope. Instead, she focused on the task at hand, clicking her heels together. "There's no place like where Jack is now. There's no place like where Jack is now."

The lights went out, and the same squeaky wheeze filled Sabrina's ears. In a split second, Charming and the girls were standing in the woods on Widow's Peak. They had little time to adjust to their new surroundings. Sabrina looked above her and saw the giant's massive foot preparing to crush them.

They managed to leap out of the way just in time, but the aftershock of the footfall tossed them around as if they were on a ship at sea.

The giant leaned down to get a better look at the three people scurrying at his feet. He reached down to snatch them, but a flaming arrow zipped from the tree line and landed in the side of the giant's face. The monster cried in pain as he plucked it from his cheek, only to have a second and third arrow pierce his chin.

Jack peeked his head out from behind some branches in a nearby tree and laughed.

"Blimey! Charming and the Grimms are on the same side? I never thought I'd live to see the day," he said. "Has the prince turned traitor like that worthless mongrel Canis?"

"The only allegiance I have is to myself," Charming said as he waved Excalibur in the air. "Now, we can do this the easy way or the hard way. But the result will be the same. You're going back to jail."

"Sorry, Prince Charming, but I've spent my last day in the Ferryport Landing lockup. My fans await," Jack said.

"We're never going to let the world see what you've been up to."

Jack fired several more arrows into the giant's face, landing a painful shot to the monster's lower lip. The giant raged as he tried to pluck it out. While the giant was busy, the young man dropped out of the tree and landed as nimbly as a cat.

"Luckily, it's easy to get your hands on another camera. I've got one hidden in the trees right now, capturing my bravery for the world to see." He loaded another arrow into his bow and fired it at the giant. It pierced the skin between two fingers of the giant's left hand, and he shrieked. Overcome with rage, the giant swept his arm across the tops of the forest trees, cracking many ancient cedars in half. A sizable chunk of one fell from the sky and nearly hit Charming in the head.

"Oh, he's angry now." The giant killer laughed, loading his bow again. This time he aimed his arrow at Charming. "But before the show can start I have to take care of a few troublesome details."

He released his arrow, and the girls watched it soar through the air at Charming. Daphne screamed and squeezed her sister's hand, knowing Jack's aim was true. But something happened the girls didn't expect. Charming lifted Excalibur slightly, and the arrow bounced off its metal blade and fell to the ground. Jack was flabbergasted.

"What luck you have!" he cried.

"Try again and see if it was luck," the prince said, stepping forward with the sword.

With hands like lightning, Jack fired another arrow, and Charming deflected it with similar results. Jack pulled three arrows from his quill and lined them up together on his bow. He fired them all at the same time. Sabrina watched in amazement as Charming guided Excalibur to block each arrow from its deadly course. Every save brought him a step closer to the villain.

"I can do this all night," Jack bragged.

Charming reached back and swung a fist at Jack's face. Sabrina was sure she saw a tooth fly out of the Englishman's mouth when he tumbled to the ground. The mayor stood over him with his sword glinting in the moonlight.

"It's over, Jack," Charming said. "It's over."

Just then the giant's monstrous hand swung down and hit the mayor from behind. Excalibur was knocked free of his grip and fell at Sabrina's feet. Charming was sent sailing through the forest, landing painfully against a tree trunk and slumping to the ground.

Jack scampered to his feet and pulled more arrows from his quill, lit them with a lighter Sabrina recognized from Granny's kitchen, and fired five off with furious speed. Each landed in more of the giant's sensitive spots. The painful barrage was enough to get the giant to back off, giving the young man an opportunity to turn on the girls. He put another arrow into his bow and aimed it at Sabrina.

Instinctively, Sabrina reached down and snatched Excalibur from the ground. It was incredibly heavy and bulky, but she swung it around in the air the best she could.

"And what do you think you're going to do with that, duck?" Jack scoffed as he stepped toward her. "Grimms aren't killers. You don't have it in you!"

"Well, we're kind of new at this job. If we break a couple of rules, that just goes with the learning process," Sabrina said with as much bravery as she could muster. Her courage was short-lived. As Jack got closer, she noticed something painted on his shirt. It was a red handprint, just like the one the police had found in her parent's abandoned car. It sent a chill through her body.

"You're the Scarlet Hand. You took my parents," Sabrina said.

Jack looked down at the red mark and smiled. "No, girl, I didn't. But I know who did."

"Where are they?" Daphne cried.

"The Scarlet Hand has plans for them," he said with a sinister laugh.

"You know, I grew up reading about you," Sabrina said, trying to keep Jack busy. "You had a very exciting life. You climbed a beanstalk, killed a giant, and captured his treasure. Lots of kids think of you as a hero."

"But not you?"

"Once, but not now. Now that I've met you—the real Jack—I see you for what you are. You're a thief and an attention seeker. It's pathetic, really. I think we should change your name to Jack the Giant Jerk."

"I don't need a magic sword to shut you up," he threatened.

Jack pulled his bowstring back farther and, just as he was about to fire his arrow, the giant's foot came down on top of him, giving the man only a split second to leap out of the way. Daphne grabbed her sister's hand, and together they raced into the forest, dodging trees and branches. Jack followed closely behind, and worse, the giant strode after him. Its first step landed several yards from them.

An arrow whizzed by and wedged itself into a nearby tree.

"That was a warning shot, ladies," the young man shouted as he loaded another arrow. "I'm quite good with this thing."

Suddenly the two girls were slipping down the side of a hill and into an ice-cold creek. Another arrow splashed in the water at Sabrina's feet as they pulled themselves out of the stream and continued to run. With now frozen feet, they did their best to avoid the jagged rocks that littered the forest floor, but soon Sabrina took a tumble and fell end over end across the ground. She tried to stand up, and quickly realized she was missing something. Her left shoe—Dorothy's left slipper—lay glistening in the moonlight behind her. It had fallen off.

"C'mon," Daphne begged as she tried to help her big sister up, but Sabrina crawled desperately toward the shoe. It was their only chance of finding their parents. She used her arms to pull herself along the ground, knowing that Jack could hit her with an arrow at any second. But before she could reach the shoe, the giant's foot came down hard on top of it. The vibrations shook the girls and sent them tumbling. When the giant lifted his foot, the shoe was gone; the only thing remaining was a sparkle of dust in the air.

Heartbroken, Sabrina pulled her sister behind a huge oak tree.

"Don't worry. I'll think of something," she said, squeezing her sister's hand.

But with a monstrous rending sound and a rain of splintered wood and soil, the tree they crouched next to was violently uprooted. The two girls looked up into the face of death towering above them and felt the giant's hot, pungent breath blow their hair back from their scalps.

What's happened to our lives? Sabrina wondered.

The giant tossed the tree aside and then reached down with his grubby hand to pick them up—but just as he did, Sabrina thrust Excalibur into the air. The giant's hand plunged into its blade, and suddenly his eyes lit up in surprise.

"What was that?" he asked softly. He stood up as if he were in a daze, unsure even of where he was. The anger in his face melted away, replaced by a sort of calm curiosity, and he began to wobble on his feet. Unable to keep his balance, he toppled over, landing flat on his back and crushing an acre of forest beneath him. A thick cloud of dust rose above his body and settled down all around them. Half a pound of soil landed in Sabrina's blond hair.

And then all was still.

"I didn't mean for that to happen," Sabrina said, looking in horror at the sword still clutched in her hand.

"Granny Relda and Mr. Canis?" Daphne whispered as tears filled her eyes.

Jack rushed through the brush and saw the giant, lying dead on the ground.

"You've killed him," he said angrily. "I was going to kill him!"

"It's over, Jack," Sabrina said.

"It's not over until I say it is," Jack raged. "I'm going to be famous again, but for another reason. Tonight, the Everafters of Ferryport Landing are going to find they are suddenly free from the spell that has kept them in this mercilessly boring town for two centuries. With your grandmum now dead, the spell turns to the last living Grimm. Some might be patient enough to wait for you two to die of old age, but I am not. Tonight I'm setting the Everafters free."

10

JACK RUSHED FORWARD AND SHOVED SABRINA to the ground. Daphne lunged at him, but she received the same treatment. Sabrina dropped Excalibur, and Jack snatched it up, admiring its blade for a moment and then readying himself to bring it down on Sabrina's head.

"They're going to have a parade in my honor for this," the young man said with a sick smile. "The Master is going to be very happy."

Suddenly a loud, wheezing honk filled the night. Jack spun around. In the giant's breast pocket, a wonderful thing appeared: Two headlights blinked to life. An engine roared and backfired violently, and then, with a squeal of tires, the Grimm family car ripped through the pocket and sped along the giant's body. At the wheel was Mr. Canis and, next to him, Granny Relda, safe and sound. The car soared over the giant's gelatinous belly, down his leg, and hit his huge kneecap, sending the car sailing into the air. It landed several yards away from Jack and the girls and skidded to a stop. The engine puttered out, the lights went dim, and the car doors opened. Granny Relda stepped out with a very concerned face.

"Jack, what is the meaning of this?" she asked.

The young man pulled the mason jar of beans out of his jacket and held it up.

"It's about this, old woman. It's about capturing my rightful place in the spotlight," Jack said.

"Those days are over," Mr. Canis said as he stepped out of the car.

"Maybe for you, traitor," Jack snarled. "But I've got bigger plans than selling shoes and measuring hemlines. These beans are going to make me a hero again. But for that to happen, some things have to change around here."

"What are you suggesting?" Granny Relda asked.

"The Grimms have to die."

"You know I won't allow that, Jack," Mr. Canis said.

"I've been killing giants since I was a lad. I suspect I won't have too much trouble with an old mutt like you."

Mr. Canis looked to Granny Relda. Something passed between them—a sort of question only the two of them understood. Granny Relda nodded, and Mr. Canis took off his hat. He smiled in a way Sabrina could only describe as eager. Once again, she was sure he was doomed. The old man had managed to take out three overweight goons, but could he handle a lightning-fast slayer of giants carrying a sword that killed anything the blade touched?

Jack charged wildly, screaming, but before he could even swing the deadly sword, a change came over Mr. Canis. His shirt ripped off his chest as his body doubled in size. His feet snapped and stretched as they transformed into paws. Hair sprang from every inch of skin; fangs crept down over his lips; his nose extended out, becoming a snarling snout; and his ears twisted into points and rose to the top of his head. But most disturbing were his eyes, which changed into the achingly bright blue color Sabrina had noticed in the family pictures. Why hadn't she guessed it before? Mr. Canis was an Everafter, and maybe the scariest one of them all. He was the Big Bad Wolf.

"If you want to sic your dog on me, Grimm, then do it. But I'll have my destiny either way," Jack said, putting the jar of beans back into his jacket and swinging Excalibur around menacingly. "I've been waiting for this for a very long time."

The Wolf charged at Jack and sent him hurtling backward into a tree, giving the young man no time to recover. The beast savagely sank his teeth into the giant killer's right arm, and Jack screamed in agony. With the Wolf on top of him, he couldn't swing the deadly sword. The best he could do was hit the beast on the head with Excalibur's handle. The Wolf backed away, laughed, and licked its lips.

"Bad news for you, Jack," the Wolf barked. "This dog bites."

In the commotion, Granny held open her arms for the girls, and they ran into them.

"You didn't tell us Mr. Canis was one of them," Sabrina said.

"Oh, didn't I?" Granny said as she kept her eyes on the fight.

The Wolf lunged at Jack again, ripping his chest with his razor-sharp claws. Jack swung back and punched the beast in the face, but the Wolf just chuckled. Desperately, the young man jumped up, grabbed a tree branch, and used it to catapult himself at the Wolf. The force sent them tumbling over each other, leaving Jack on top.

"When I kill you, this town is going to erect a statue in my honor," Jack boasted.

The Wolf snarled as he rolled over on top of Jack. "I don't think this is going to turn out as you plan, little boy. Your rotting corpse will hang in the town square tonight. That is, after I've eaten all the juicy parts."

Jack thrust his knee into the Wolf 's belly, knocking the wind out of him and giving the young man the chance to throw the beast off. He crawled to his feet and picked up Excalibur.

"Even the tiniest scratch will send you on your way, mongrel," Jack warned. He rushed forward, pushed the beast against a tree, and held the lethal blade to his neck. "From now on they will call me Jack the Legend Killer!"

Sabrina looked to her grandmother and saw the worry in her face. She knew Jack was going to win, and then he would turn on them. How would the three of them fight him off? But suddenly, above the snarling and fighting, she heard an odd sound, as if someone had just played notes on a flute. At first Sabrina thought she might have imagined it, but then a swarm of pixies darted out of the woods and surrounded Jack. He cried in pain with every little sting, and soon blood began to leak from all over his body.

Puck floated down from the trees and rested on a branch above the fighting.

"Puck!" Daphne cried. "You really are a hero!"

"Hush, you'll ruin my reputation," he replied.

In vain, Jack tried to brush the pixies off, swatting at them wildly with little result and dropping the sword in his struggle.

"Old lady, are you well?" Puck asked as he floated to the ground. "I tried to tell Sabrina that Jack couldn't be trusted, but she wouldn't listen. She's very stubborn and stupid."

"I'm sure Sabrina had her reasons, Puck," Granny replied as she winked at her granddaughter. "But before we can celebrate, Jack has a jar in his coat we need."

Puck smiled, took out his flute, and played a quick, sharp note. One pixie left the others and buzzed around the boy's head.

"We need to get that jar away from him," Puck said. The little light blinked as if to say yes and zipped into the storm of pixies tormenting Jack. Suddenly a small group of them flew into his jacket and collectively carried the jar of magic beans away.

"No!" Jack cried in panic, swatting and swinging wildly at the pixies. Seeing his prize carried off, he desperately grasped for the jar, only managing to knock it to the ground, sending shards of glass and beans in all directions.

"Oh, dear," Granny gasped. "Mr. Canis, we have a problem."

The Wolf fell over as if he were having a fight with himself.

"I'm not going back inside, old man!" the beast bellowed. He groaned and complained as he transformed back into Mr. Canis. The old man looked exhausted and broken. He wore a worried expression. "He tasted blood."

"I know, and we will deal with that soon. Right now we have to get the children out of here," Granny Relda said. Unfortunately, most of her words were drowned out by a horrible rumbling. The little white beans were taking root. They dug deep into the forest's soil, and instantly a hundred little green sprouts popped out of the ground. The sprouts grew at an alarming rate, becoming vines and then stalks that jockeyed for space. They soared higher and higher into the air until it seemed they would touch the moon itself.

"What have you done?" Jack bellowed.

"You wanted giants, Jack. You're going to get your wish,"

Granny Relda said as the first giant came crawling down a stalk, planting a foot on the forest floor. Dozens and dozens followed, nearly a hundred in all, knocking over trees planted centuries ago. Each one of the giants was uglier than the last, and all of them had murder in their eyes. One of the most gnarled of the bunch stepped forward. It let out an ear-shattering blast and pounded its chest.

"Fe, fi, fo, fum, I smell the blood of that murderous Englishman!" the giant thundered at Jack, sending his hair flapping behind him.

"I didn't kill your brother—it was the girl!" Jack cried, pointing a shaky finger at Sabrina. "Sabrina Grimm killed him!"

The giants looked down at Sabrina with suspicious eyes. One ducked his head down, shoving it into the girls' faces. His nostrils blasted hot air into their clothes.

"Lies!" the giant bellowed, spraying Sabrina and Daphne with its hot, snotty breath. "These are children. They could not kill one of us!"

Trembling with terror, Sabrina stepped forward. "No, it's true. I did it. I killed him. It was an accident. I didn't mean to do it. I was fighting Jack, and your brother was hurt. I'm sorry."

"See, I told you!" Jack cried. "She's the guilty one."

The giant swooped down and grabbed Jack in his huge, grimy hand.

"You set the events in motion, Englishman. You will pay for the crime!" the giant bellowed.

Granny Relda stepped forward. "What do you plan on doing with him?" she asked.

"Crush his bones to make our bread." The giant grunted. "Or maybe we will pull his little limbs off one by one and see if he screams."

"You'll do nothing of the sort," Granny Relda replied. "Take him to your queen. She'll decide what to do with him."

"Who are you to tell us what to do?" the giant raged.

"I'm Relda Grimm," Granny said. "If you don't know me, your queen will."

The giants grumbled to one another until their leader bowed his head in respect.

"Help me, Relda!" Jack cried. "Don't let them take me!"

Granny Relda lowered her eyes. "I cannot deny them their justice. I only hope they are more merciful with you than you have been with them."

Jack saw the futility of his words and calmed himself. Then he laughed, almost insanely. "Do you think I did this all on my own?" he ranted. "Where do you think I got the first magic bean? The Scarlet Hand is coming, and your days are numbered! The Master has Henry and Veronica, and you're next!"

The giants ignored Jack's taunts and turned back toward their beanstalks. A few leaned down and gingerly picked up their dead brother. They carried him on their shoulders as they climbed back up into the sky.

"Granny, stop them. Jack knows who took our mom and dad," Sabrina begged.

Granny shook her head.

"It's too late, Sabrina."

The giants disappeared into the cold night air just as three squad cars roared into the clearing with lights and sirens. Flying high above the police were Glinda in her bubble and Frau Pfefferkuchenhaus on her broom. They sent streams of fire at the beanstalks, setting them ablaze.

Hamstead got out of his car and, along with Boarman and Swineheart, rushed to the family's side.

"I'm glad you're OK, Relda," the sheriff said.

"Thank you very much, Sheriff," Granny replied. "It has been a difficult couple days."

"You've got some pretty smart grandchildren," Hamstead said, smiling at Sabrina and Daphne. "Maybe a little *too* smart. They're not ones to let a man explain anything, and not so easy on my wardrobe, but I shouldn't be surprised with a last name like Grimm."

He reached his hand out, and Sabrina shook it. Daphne did the same.

"In the future, kids, remember, we're the good guys," Hamstead said. "If you'll excuse me, I have to confiscate a little evidence."

The sheriff looked at Mr. Canis and nodded his head.

"Wolf," he said with an odd respect.

"Pig," Canis replied.

"Relda, your grandchildren are as meddlesome as you are," Charming said as he entered the clearing. He was rubbing his head and placing his phone back in his pocket. "But they were helpful in putting an end to Jack's plan."

"Your Majesty," Relda chirped happily, "are you suggesting that the Grimms might be useful in this town?"

"Hardly," Charming growled. He turned to the girls and looked at them darkly. "Remember what I said about tomorrow, children."

He spun around and made a beeline for the sheriff.

Daphne and Sabrina hugged their grandmother around the waist and burst into a torrent of happy tears. Granny Relda returned their affection with a hundred kisses.

"*Lieblings*, are you OK?" she asked at last.

This time, Sabrina didn't pull away from the old woman. This time, Granny's hug felt like home.

"I'm OK," Sabrina said, fighting back more tears.

"We're sorry we almost got you killed," Daphne said. "We're not very good detectives."

"Nonsense!" Granny Relda laughed as she led them to the car. "You rescued Mr. Canis and me and managed to prevent a serious catastrophe. I say the two of you are first-rate detectives. We should celebrate. Does anyone have any ideas?"

Sabrina eased back into her seat. "I'd really just like to get out of these clothes," she said, looking down at the monkey hanging from the tree on her sweatshirt.

HANG IN THERE, it read.

Elvis woke the girls the next morning with loving licks on their faces. Luckily, Jack had not hurt the dog too badly. His ribs were bruised, and he would have to wear a bandage on his side until the veterinarian could remove his stitches. He had a big plastic cone around his head to prevent him from licking his wound, and everywhere he walked he knocked piles of things onto the floor. The only thing that seemed to truly hurt was Elvis's pride. Daphne apologized to him for not paying attention to his clue and promised that his opinion would always be considered in the future.

Granny greeted them at the dining room table with more of her unusual culinary treats. That morning, they enjoyed blue scrambled eggs, some little orange nuts, home-fried potatoes soaked in sparkly green gravy, and wedges of tomato. Mr. Canis didn't join them.

"Is Mr. Canis OK?" Daphne asked.

"He will be," Granny Relda replied. "I'm sure he'll be happy to hear you are concerned."

"Where's Puck?" Sabrina asked, more out of suspicion that he would spring out of nowhere than real worry.

Granny Relda smiled. "He'll be here soon."

After breakfast, the three Grimms went to the mall. Granny Relda bought the girls a dozen outfits apiece and found a new hat with a sunflower on it for herself. Sabrina suggested they burn their orange monkey sweatshirts and blue heart-covered pants, but Daphne refused.

"Mr. Canis did his best, girls," Granny explained. "He is color-blind, after all."

When they got home, Granny had presents for them. The girls unwrapped them quickly and found their own brand-new, leather-bound journals, just like the ones their entire family used to record the events they witnessed. The covers were stenciled in gold with the words FAIRY-TALE ACCOUNTS and each of their names. When Sabrina opened hers, she found hundreds of blank pages.

"Like your father and generations of Grimms before him, it is your responsibility to put on paper what you see, so that the future generations may be prepared," Granny said. "We are Grimms. This is what we do."

The rest of the day, the girls scribbled in the books. They picked each other's brains for anything they might have forgotten, and when they were finished, Sabrina tucked the picture of her family inside her journal's pages. Together, the girls rushed downstairs and placed their books alongside their father's journal.

"Girls, I'd like to show you something else," Granny said.

The girls followed her up the stairs, where she unlocked Mirror's room. The little man's face appeared in the glass, and he smiled when the old woman and the girls entered.

"Good afternoon, Relda," Mirror said.

"Good afternoon. I do hope you are feeling better," Granny replied.

"Much better. The bruises look worse than they feel," Mirror said.

"That's nice to know," the old woman said. She turned to the girls and took their hands. "Would you like to see your parents?"

Sabrina's heart nearly jumped from her chest. "Yes, please."

Granny turned back to the mirror. "Mirror, mirror, near and far," she said aloud. "Show us where their parents are."

The mirror misted over and two figures slowly appeared in the reflection. When the mist cleared, Sabrina saw her parents, Henry and Veronica, lying on a bed in a dark room. They were very still, with their eyes closed.

"They're dead," Sabrina said before she could stop herself.

"No, not dead," Granny Relda corrected her. "Just sleeping.

They appear to be the victims of a magic spell. As far as I can tell, they are safe and healthy."

"We lost one of Dorothy's slippers," Daphne cried. "We could have used them to rescue Mom and Dad."

Sabrina's face flushed with regret.

"*Liebling*, don't you think I have tried the slippers and everything else inside the mirror?" Granny Relda sighed. "This Scarlet Hand, whoever they are, used strong magic to take your mom and dad away from us, but we aren't going to give up. We'll find them, I promise."

The girls wrapped their arms around Granny Relda and hugged her tightly. Sabrina and Daphne sobbed, both tears of happiness that their parents were alive and tears of despair that they didn't know where they were.

Suddenly there was a knock on the door to the house. The old woman took a handkerchief from her handbag and wiped the girls' eyes. Then she wiped her own and stuffed the hankie back in her purse.

"Come, girls, we have guests," she said as she exited the room. The girls watched the image of their parents slowly fade from the mirror and then stood for a moment, staring at their own reflections.

"We're home now," Sabrina said to her sister. "No more running away."

"Well, duh!" Daphne giggled.

The two left the room and closed the door behind them. Then they ran down the stairs to the foyer. Puck was already inside, carrying several boxes filled to the top with old toys, junk, and several dead fish. Behind him were Glinda, Hamstead, Boarman, and Swineheart. The group walked past them into the dining room and spread a huge roll of papers onto the table. When Sabrina got a closer look, she realized they were blueprints.

"What are the police doing here?" Sabrina asked.

"We're not here in an official capacity. We're putting an addition on your house," Hamstead said as his expression turned to a sly smile. "This house isn't big enough. You need another bedroom right away. Relda asked us to do the job. Before we went into law enforcement, we were in construction."

"I'm getting my own room?" Sabrina squealed happily.

Daphne looked insulted and stuck out her tongue.

"Oh, Sabrina, we're not building you your own bedroom yet," Granny apologized. "No, we need another room because—"

"I'm moving in!" Puck interrupted. He shoved his box of junk into Sabrina's hands and joined the witch and the deputies looking over the plans, declaring that they needed to add a dungeon and a throne room.

"He's lying, right?" Sabrina asked hopefully. "You wouldn't let that stinky freak move in here with us?"

"I think it's great!" Daphne cried.

"Girls, he may not be my real grandson," Granny replied, "but I love him like he was my own."

Daphne took her sister's hand and smiled. "I have a feeling we're going to have a lot more to write in those books."

Sabrina scowled.

ABOUT THIS BOOK

When my editor, Susan Van Metre, came to me with plans for an anniversary edition of the Sisters Grimm series, I realized I had the perfect opportunity to do something I never thought would be possible—to revisit Ferryport Landing and fix a few mistakes. Some of them were made as a result of an ambitious publication schedule, and others were the blunders of a new, inexperienced writer trying to create a world from scratch. I always wished I had a time machine so I could go back and fix the problems before they were printed. So to everyone at Amulet Books—thanks for the time machine!

Fans of this series will most likely not notice what has been altered. And some flaws I left as is—after all, this was the first book I ever wrote, the starting point in my pursuit to become a better storyteller, so it shouldn't be perfect. After all, there's no such thing as a perfect book. But this edition does make me smile—and to a writer, a smile can be all the perfection you need. I hope you enjoy my return to Granny Relda's big yellow house, to the Hall of Wonders, and to the two little girls who have given me so much joy.

ACKNOWLEDGMENTS

I'd like to thank my editor, Susan Van Metre at Amulet Books, whose guidance helped me find the book inside my idea; my agent, Alison Fargis of the Stonesong Press, for taking a chance on me; Joseph Deasy, who was honest enough to tell me when my writing could be better; my love, Alison, for telling me when Joe was wrong; Jonathan Flom, for all his support over the years; Joe Harris, for being a good friend; my parents, Michael and Wilma, for filling our house with books even when the checking account was empty; and Daisy, who was patient when I was too busy writing to take her for a walk.

ABOUT THE AUTHOR

Michael Buckley is the *New York Times*–bestselling author of the Sisters Grimm and NERDS series, *Kel Gilligan's Daredevil Stunt Show*, and the Undertow Trilogy. He has also written and developed television shows for many networks. Michael lives in Brooklyn, New York, with his wife, Alison; their son, Finn; and their dog, Friday.

A Reader's Guide

Dear Reader,

When I set out to write the adventures of the Sisters Grimm, I wanted to update everyone's favorite fairy-tale characters using adventure, humor, and surprises. I thought it would be easy. After all, I'd heard all the stories and seen all the movies. What else was there to know?

It turns out there was plenty more to know.

When I reread some of the original stories, I found that everything I thought I knew was wrong. Imagine my surprise when I discovered that the Little Mermaid didn't win her handsome prince's heart in the end. Or that Pinocchio wasn't swallowed by a whale but eaten by a shark! Or that Snow White wasn't awakened when she was kissed but when a piece of poisoned apple, stuck in her throat, was dislodged. I went back and reread all the classics, by the Brothers Grimm, Hans Christian Andersen, Lewis Carroll, Andrew Lang, Rudyard Kipling, L. Frank Baum, and dozens more. What I found was a wealth of funny, exciting, scary, and adventure-filled stories, and my hope is that the Sisters Grimm series will inspire you to do the same. Your local library should have a wide collection of fairy tales and folklore, filled with as many surprises as there are in Sabrina and Daphne's adventures. I invite you to crack open these classics and find out what you've been missing. Happy reading, and beware of the Scarlet Hand!

Michael Buckley

FAIRY TALES

Many people think fairy tales are just stories about princesses and witches that our parents tell us so we won't take candy from strangers or wander off by ourselves. But if fairy tales were only here to teach us lessons, they probably would have disappeared long ago.

Fairy tales tell us big truths about life—not just as it was in the past, but as it is today—and show us how to make our way through it with bravery, cunning, and wisdom. They are such useful guides that they've been followed for centuries, by people in every country on the globe. Two hundred years ago, a young girl fell asleep in her bed listening to the same fairy tale you liked to read when you were little.

So how did fairy tales from so long ago end up here? For a long time, fairy tales were only passed down orally. That means, basically, that they were created from a giant, centuries-long game of telephone. People told stories to children, friends, or strangers they met during their travels. Then those people told the stories to others, changing little details along the way. The general plots stayed the same, but the stories grew and changed, depending on where and when they were told. Sometimes two different versions of the same story would pop up in two different countries. The names and settings would be different, but the same things would happen. For example, there are versions of the Cinderella story in countries as far apart as Egypt and Iceland.

Following Fairy Tales

The Cinderella story is one of the most famous fairy tales in the world because it's been adapted to so many different cultures and times. The first written version appeared more than a thousand years ago in China, and new versions of the tale pop up all the time—think of all the movies you've seen about a poor, mistreated girl who ends up with the rich, handsome guy. The details change—maybe "Cinderella" works in a car wash or ropes cows—but the plot stays the same.

You can conduct your own experiment to see how fairy tales might grow or change. All you'll need is a piece of paper, a pen, and a few friends.

Have one person start writing two or three sentences on the paper to begin the Cinderella story. Then have that person fold the paper down, so only the last line he or she wrote can be seen.

Pass the paper on to the next person, who will add a few sentences to the story, with only the line before as a guide. Then the second writer should fold the paper again, so that only the last line of his or her writing is visible. Continue to pass the paper, write, and fold until you finish a page, or two if you're feeling ambitious. When you're done, unfold the paper and read the whole story through. See if you can trace how the story line and characters changed as the paper was passed from one person to another.

Grimms to the Rescue

For a long time, people told fairy tales by memory, and often stories were changed or even lost as they were passed down. That's when the Brothers Grimm stepped in. Jacob and Wilhelm Grimm grew up in Germany listening to fairy tales, and they worried that the wonderful stories they heard might be changed, lost, or forgotten. The brothers decided to write down their favorite tales so people would remember them forever. Some people think of the Grimm brothers as writers, and they were, but more than writers they were collectors—even hunters—of good stories. They talked to everyone, from their close friends to strangers they met traveling. Once, they met a poor, ragged soldier who asked for their old clothes in exchange for his stories. The Brothers Grimm were more than happy to make the trade—in fact, they probably thought they were getting the better deal!

You may have heard different versions of the same fairy tale, some scarier than others. When the Grimm brothers first wrote their stories down, they were violent tales, packed with villains who died in horrible ways. The Grimms thought that adults, especially professors and historians, would be the ones reading their stories. They were surprised when they realized that it was kids who liked their fairy tales best! So Wilhelm and Jacob rewrote their stories, making them more poetic and a little less violent. But they didn't take everything out, because they knew that being scared was part of the fun of reading fairy tales. They didn't want to cheat their younger readers of a good story.

The Basic Ingredients

It seems that an awful lot of fairy tales are full of wicked witches, endangered princesses, and handsome princes who save the day. That's because putting together a fairy tale is kind of like putting together a potion, and different stories use many of the same ingredients. What does a good fairy tale need? Here's a list of some of the most common elements:

- Heroes/good characters
- Villains/very, very bad characters
- Interesting sidekicks
- A journey or quest
- Magic
- A happy ending

Can you think of any other important components of a good fairy tale?

Do you think all of these components are necessary for a good story?

Some fairy tales, like many of the stories written by Hans Christian Andersen, don't end happily. Others, like some more modern renditions of old fairy tales, don't include magic.

As you read the Sisters Grimm series, look for elements from the list above and see how many you can find. Think of Sabrina, Daphne, and Granny Relda as heroes (or "damsels in distress," sometimes). Who are the villains? Do you ever feel sorry for them? Think about different ways in which the Sisters Grimm books imitate or challenge the typical fairy-tale formula.

Crime Watch

The Grimm sisters are "sleuths of fairy-tale crime." It's a good thing, too, because there seem to be an awful lot of crimes committed in fairy tales. Without the three little (or not so little) pigs out patrolling the streets, crime was rampant throughout many classic fairy tales. Below are some well-known fairy tales and a list of crimes. Can you connect the crime with the story, and bring the perpetrators to justice like the Grimm sisters?

Crime Watch

A) Goldilocks and the Three Bears	1) Lying
B) Little Red Riding Hood	2) Identity theft
C) Beauty and the Beast	3) Destruction of property
D) Snow White	4) Child labor
E) Rumpelstiltskin	5) Hostage-taking
F) Cinderella	6) Attempted murder
G) The Three Little Pigs	7) Breaking and entering

Answers:

A-7 (Goldilocks enters the house of the three bears uninvited)

B-2 (the wolf pretends to be Red Riding Hood's grandma)

C-5 (the Beast makes Beauty stay in his castle and will not let her leave)

D-6 (the evil queen tries to kill Snow White four times)

E-1 (the girl's father lies and tells the king that she can spin gold out of straw)

F-4 (the evil stepmother and her daughters make young Cinderella their slave)

G-3 (the wolf destroys the pigs' houses)

Be the Next Grimm

Not everybody may get the chance to hang out with Everafters and solve fairy-tale crimes like the Grimm sisters, but anyone can follow in the Grimm brothers' famous storytelling tradition. Because most fairy tales follow a pretty simple formula, it's surprisingly easy to create your own. See if you can use some common building blocks to write your own story.

Here are a few questions to get you started thinking:

Who is my hero?

Who is my villain?

Is there a trusty sidekick?

Where does my story take place?

What does my hero want?

What is he or she looking for?

What challenges must my hero overcome?

Once you decide what you're writing about, here are some phrases to help you put your ideas all together:

Once upon a time . . .

There once was a boy . . .

Many, many years ago there lived . . .

Now, you shall hear a story that somebody's great-great-grandmother told a little girl many years ago . . .

. . . and ________________ *was in grave danger . . .*

. . . but ________________ *was too smart to be tricked, and decided to . . .*

. . . and they lived happily ever after!

. . . snip, snap, snout. This tale's told out.

Remember, part of the fun of fairy tales is being surprised, so be as creative as you can. Boys don't always have to rescue girls, and villains don't always have to be wicked old women (think about the surprising heroes and villains in the Sisters Grimm books). After you finish your fairy tale, try reading it out loud to see how it sounds. You'll be working in the great, centuries-old tradition of Jacob and Wilhelm Grimm!

Test Your Fairy-Tale Smarts

Think you have the smarts to be part of the Grimm family? As Granny Relda teaches, there's lots to learn. See how much you know by taking the following quiz about your favorite tales!

1. The seven dwarfs make an agreement with Snow White allowing her to stay with them if in return she will . . .

a. stand around looking pretty

b. teach them how to wash all the dust off their mining clothes

c. cook, clean, and keep house

d. accompany them to the mines every day and sing while they work.

2. At the very end of Little Red Riding Hood, the wolf's stomach is filled with . . .

a. Granny's famous chicken wings

b. Granny

c. absolutely nothing

d. stones

Test Your Fairy-Tale Smarts

3. Before the queen guesses Rumpelstiltskin's real name, she guesses two others, including . . .

a. Harry

b. Joshua

c. Jack

d. Prince Charming

4. The evil sorceress who finds Hansel and Gretel plans to . . .

a. feed them her leftovers forever

b. make them clean her house all day long

c. hold them hostage until their parents pay for them

d. eat them

5. Rapunzel is raised by an evil enchantress to punish her parents for . . .

a. exiling the enchantress from their kingdom

b. stealing some plants from the enchantress's garden

c. having the fairest daughter in all the land

d. not taking their daughter to get a haircut when she clearly needs one

Answers: 1-c, 2-d, 3-a, 4-d, 5-b

The Grimm Web

You can find out more about the Brothers Grimm and their stories at these Internet sites:

Brothers Grimm: Fairy Tales, History, Facts, and More
www.nationalgeographic.com/grimm
National Geographic presents twelve tales from the famous brothers in their original form. Open the treasure chest to find a map of the Fairy-Tale Road through Germany, *National Geographic* articles on the Brothers Grimm, links to other Grimm resources, and more.

Grimm Fairy Tales
www.grimmfairytales.com/en/main
Interactive, narrated, animated versions of several fairy tales plus biographical information, games, and other fun stuff from Kids Fun Canada.

The SurLaLune Fairy-Tales Site
www.surlalunefairytales.com
This personal website hosted by a librarian serves as a portal to fairy-tale and folklore studies, featuring forty-four annotated fairy tales, with their histories, cross-cultural tales, and illustrations.

ENJOY THIS
SNEAK PEEK FROM

THE SISTERS GRIMM 2

THE UNUSUAL SUSPECTS

1

LET'S GET THIS PARTY STARTED, ALREADY!" Sabrina grumbled as she rubbed another cramp out of her leg. For the last three nights she and her seven-year-old sister, Daphne, had been crouching behind a stack of Diaper Rash Donna dolls waiting for criminals to rob Gepetto's Toyshop. She was tired, hungry, and more than a little irritated. She should have been at home, sleeping in her own bed, not using a board game as a pillow.

"Shhh! You'll wake him," Daphne said, pointing to their two-hundred-pound Great Dane. Elvis was lying next to a display of yo-yos, sound asleep. Sabrina couldn't help but envy him.

"Girls, you have to be quiet," Granny Relda said as she huddled behind some foam rubber footballs. "The crooks could come at any second!"

In most ordinary towns, the police do not rely on two kids and a sleeping dog to solve crimes, but Ferryport Landing was no ordinary town. More than half of its residents were part of a secret community known as Everafters. Everafters were actually fairy-tale characters who had migrated from far and wide to the United States over two hundred years ago. They had settled in the little town and now used magical disguises to live and work alongside their human neighbors. Ogres worked at the post office, witches ran the twenty-four-hour diner, and the legendary Prince Charming served as the town's mayor. The humans were none the wiser—except the Grimms.

Sabrina would have been happy to live in blissful ignorance, but her family had been involved with Everafters since her great-great-great-great-grandfather Wilhelm Grimm and his brother, Jacob, helped establish Ferryport Landing. Some might think it thrilling to live next door to fairies and princesses, but Sabrina felt like she was trapped inside a bad dream. Most of the Everafters saw her family as their bitter enemies, largely because of the magical curse Wilhelm and a witch named Baba Yaga had used to trap them within the town's borders. It stopped a war between the Everafters and the humans, but it also created an invisible cage. No Everafter could leave Ferryport Landing unless the Grimms abandoned the town or died out. More than a few folks would have been happy to see either happen.

Even with that dark cloud hanging over her family, Granny Relda had made a few genuine friends in the community. Among them was a portly sheriff named Ernest Hamstead, who happened to be one of the three not-so-little pigs. He occasionally turned up at the family's door asking for help with unsolved cases, and Granny couldn't resist a mystery.

So here Sabrina sat, leg cramps and all, waiting for burglars to make their move inside the toyshop. There were things she would rather be doing, things she should be doing, like finding her parents. Instead, she and her sister were hiding behind Etch-A-Sketches and cans of Silly String stacked miles high. It was boring work with few distractions. At least she could use the time productively. Sabrina reached into her pocket and pulled out a small flashlight. She flicked its switch to illuminate a book sitting at her feet. She picked it up and started reading. *The Jungle Book* might hold a clue to rescuing her mom and dad, but she'd barely read a paragraph before Daphne was grumbling.

"Sabrina," Daphne whispered, "what are you doing? You're going to give us away. Turn off that light."

Sabrina slammed the book closed. There was no arguing with her sister. Daphne had taken to all this silly detective work the way a dog takes to a slice of bologna. Like their grandmother, Daphne loved all of it—the note taking, the stakeouts, the endless research. If only she would use all that energy on something that really mattered—reuniting their family!

A rustling sound drifted across the room, and Sabrina quickly shut off her flashlight. She peered over the stack of dolls and spotted something moving near a display for a hot holiday toy called Don't Tickle the Tiger. Daphne poked her head up, too.

"Do you see anything?" she whispered.

"No. But it's coming from that direction," Sabrina whispered back, pointing toward the rustling. "Wake up Sleepy and see if he smells anything."

Daphne shook Elvis until he staggered to his feet. The big dog's bandages had only recently been removed. He'd had a run-in with a bad guy's boot but had made a full recovery. Still, he was a bit sluggish. He looked around as if he didn't remember where he was.

"You smell any bad guys, Elvis?" Daphne asked softly.

The dog sniffed the air, and his eyes grew wide. He let out a soft whine. The best nose in the Hudson Valley smelled something, indeed.

"Go get 'em, boy!" Daphne cried, and the Great Dane took off like a rocket.

Unfortunately, that was when Sabrina realized Elvis's leash was wrapped around her foot. As the dog howled wildly and tore through the store, he dragged Sabrina, thrashing, behind him, knocking over stacks of board games and sending balls bouncing in every direction. They emptied puzzle pieces everywhere and sent an army of Slinkys slinking across the floor. Sabrina struggled to grab the leash, but every time she got close to freeing herself, the dog took a wild turn and sent her skidding. She slid into a pile of what felt like sticky leaves. Some clung to her arms and legs, and one glued itself to her forehead.

"Turn on the lights!" Daphne shouted.

When the lights finally came on, Elvis stopped, stood over Sabrina, and barked. The girl sat up and then looked down at herself. She was covered in sticky glue mousetraps, each of which had a tiny little man, no more than a couple of inches high, stuck fast in the glue.

"Hey, let me go!" one of them shouted.

"What's the big idea?" another cried.

"Lilliputians! I knew it!" Granny Relda said, then spotted Sabrina's predicament and laughed. When Sabrina scowled at her, she tried to stop but couldn't.

"Oh, *liebling*," she giggled.

"Who's the sick psychopath who came up with this idea?" one of the Lilliputians shouted indignantly.

Granny leaned down to him and smiled. "Don't worry, with a little vegetable oil we'll have you free in no time."

"But I'm afraid you're under arrest," Sheriff Hamstead said as he stepped out from behind a rack of doll clothes. His puffy, pink face beamed proudly as he tugged his trousers up over his massive belly.

The Lilliputians groaned and complained as the sheriff went to work yanking the sticky traps off Sabrina's clothes.

"You have the right to remain silent. Anything you say can and will be used against you in a court of law."

"Ouch!" said Sabrina as the sheriff tugged a glue-trap from her forehead.

"I'm not talking, copper," one of the Lilliputians snapped. "And I'm suing you for wrongful arrest."

"Wrongful arrest!" Sheriff Hamstead exclaimed. Unfortunately, when the portly policeman got angry or excited, the magical disguise he used to hide who he really was stopped working. Now his nose vanished and was replaced by a runny pink snout. Two hairy pig ears popped out of the top of his head, and a series of snorts, squeals, and huffs came out of his mouth. Hamstead had nearly completed the change when the security guard from the next store over wandered into the chaos.

"What's going on in here?" the guard asked with a tough, authoritative voice. He was a tall, husky man with a military-style haircut, but when he saw the pig in a police uniform hovering over a dozen tiny men in glue traps, he nearly fainted.

"Oh, dear. We forgot some of the shops have their own security guards," Granny Relda said softly as she reached into her handbag and approached the stunned man.

"Granny, no," Sabrina begged.

"I don't have a choice, Sabrina. It doesn't hurt him," Granny explained, then blew some soft pink dust into the guard's face.

His eyes glazed over as the old woman told him he'd had another ordinary night at work and nothing unusual had occurred. The security guard nodded in agreement.

"Another night at work," he mumbled, falling under the forgetful dust's magic.

Sabrina scowled. She hated when magic was the quick-fix to a problem, especially when the problem involved humans.